# MINNA'S STORY
# 1895-1898

EVERY MAN WILL GO WITH THEE BE THY GVIDE

IN THY MOST NEED TO GO BY THY SIDE

## THE SECRET
## LOVE OF DR.
## SIGMUND FREUD

*by* KATHLEEN DANIELS

# MINNA'S STORY

Published by
Health Press
P.O. Drawer 1388
Santa Fe, New Mexico 87504

Library of Congress Cataloging-in-Publication Data

Daniels, Kathleen, 1961–
Minna's story: the secret love of Dr. Sigmund Freud/Kathleen Daniels.

       p.        cm.
Includes bibliographical references.
ISBN 0-929173-08-2
1. Freud, Sigmund, 1856–1939—Fiction. 2. Bernays, Minna—Fiction. I. Title.
PS3554.A56365M56   1992
813'.54 — dc2090- 47259

                                        CIP

To Dr. Zvi Lothane

and

To Minna, who has been silent long enough

# Publisher's Note

For many years, there have been speculations made about the nature of the relationship between Sigmund Freud and his sister-in-law, Minna Bernays. It has long been suggested that they were lovers and confidantes and even that Minna conceived Freud's child and underwent an abortion. These theories have been fueled from valid sources, such as Carl Jung, who stated that Minna, in a fit of distress, confessed a sexual relationship with Freud. Freudian scholars appear divided on the issue of the nature of their relationship.

This work must be considered fact-based fiction – drawn from actual events, dates, and circumstances taken from Freud's letters and biographies but with fictional dialogue. Living in Vienna just blocks from the old Freud household while researching this book, the author retraced the documented travels of Freud and Minna, trying to provide authentic details, down to hotel names, whenever possible.

One thing is for certain. Minna Bernays *did* live with the Freud family for many years and was working closely with Freud for at least ten of those years translating, proofreading, and editing manuscripts, as well as accompanying him in travel.

Because of the intimate nature of their relationship, Minna has been all but obliterated from Sigmund Freud's family history. Certain documents and pictures are sealed until well after the year 2000 in accordance with the wishes of Anna Freud, his daughter. The truth about Minna and Freud's relationship remains with these documents.

# *Prologue*

How the diary found its way into my hands is a strange-enough tale. At the time, I was living in Vienna at the Pension Andreas, the equivalent to an American boardinghouse. My small room overlooked the Floriangasse, an old winding street near the ornate Josephinum on Wahringerstrasse. I was studying at the University of Vienna Medical School on a fellowship and in the cool mornings frequented the Café Merkur, where I could warm myself with a mélange coffee and roll before my daily studies.

On that day—November 9, 1980—I left the medical school early and, not yet ready to face the emptiness of my modest room, meandered along looking in all the shop windows, especially admiring the flowers in the local Blumer. At last I went to the Café Landtman to order espresso and to scan the Austrian *Kurier* and the *International Herald Tribune*. America and everything familiar seemed very far away.

Vienna, a highly political city, has never been particularly welcoming to newcomers. I had established several friendly relationships at the medical school but had yet to find someone with whom I truly felt at ease. When evening fell, however, it was obvious that Vienna was a city for lovers. The soft lights and strains of music pouring forth from every doorway were enjoyed by couples strolling arm in arm. Due to painful memories of a disastrous relationship left behind, I was generally more comfortable exploring my temporary home in the daytime, and I seldom ventured out at night.

I was deeply in love with an attractive, intelligent man, but he was married. Although he pledged his love to me, he could not leave his wife —a demanding, shrewish sort of woman. When the opportunity to travel to Vienna arose early that fall, I had accepted the position quickly, welcoming the break from my lonely life and hoping that geographically distancing myself from him would remove his traces from my consciousness, help me to forget the strong lines of his face, the scent of his body, and erase the sinking feeling I had whenever I thought of him with his wife.

My modest room at the pension was small and a bit threadbare, but as a temporary dwelling, it suited my needs. As for food, the evening meals were sufficient, consisting of the basic meat, dumplings, and potatoes. Comfortable as I was, though, I had a feeling that something important was missing. I was simply marking time until some undefinable event I could not even imagine arrived.

That fateful afternoon, I finished my espresso and newspapers and wandered out to the street. The Café Landtman was near the Burgtheatre and was frequented by the well-dressed before- and after-theatre crowd. The "Burg," as it was called, has a smiling statue that stands above the door, and I was impressed by the grandeur of this elegant theatre that had catered to emperors. A revival piece by Arthur Schnitzler – that famous Austrian dramatist – was planned for the evening, but the state of my finances helped me to resist.

Then, as I crossed Dr. Karl Lueger Ring, one of the major arteries of the Ringstrasse that encircles the old city, I suddenly felt a need to hurry, one of those mysterious feelings that repels logic. Dodging the yellow-and-green trams, I strode briskly past the Rathaus, the city hall, down Grillparzer Strasse, and then ran across Landesgerichts Strasse, a perilous course at best.

As I hurried on up the Floriangasse toward my pension, something made me stop abruptly before an old bookstore that I had passed many times. The window was crammed with antiques, tattered books, old statues of Emperor Franz Josef, and other knickknacks from the last hundreds of years. Drawn as a moth to flame, I was impelled to step inside. After my eyes had adjusted to the dim light, I noticed the proprietor, Walter Amend, an older, heavyset man, emptying boxes of pictures and books, which he explained had recently been purchased at auction. I noted some of the interesting old titles and asked permission to look through some of his other treasures.

Through a low doorway there was a small, musty room piled high with battered, watermarked cartons. A single cracked and dingy window let in what was left of daylight. As I was in no hurry to return to my lonely pension, I cleared a place upon the floor and idly began to sort through the nearest box. Very soon an unusual feeling of anticipation came over me. Although the first box had not revealed any book or artifact of unusual interest, I dragged a second carton toward me. Just at that moment, the last weak rays of sunlight trickled in through the dirty window and illuminated a water-stained box tucked away in a corner of the room. I would like to report that the box was surrounded by a mystical cloud or some other such portent, but in reality, I was reluctant to put my hand into this old and musty receptacle, where I assumed it might well encounter spiders or some other such noxious creatures. I gingerly reached in and extracted a weathered and decrepit volume of about three hundred pages with a stained brown cover. After I dusted it off with my sleeve, I saw the words *Die Traumdeutung* on the front page. The book had been published in 1900 by Franz Deuticke, Leipzig and Wien [ Vienna], and with a jolt of surprise, I saw the author's name – *Dr. Sigm. Freud*. An inscription on the inside front cover read, in a sprawling hand, *To Minna: A Source of Inspiration*, and was dated October 27, 1899.

The other books in the box were of little note except for *Sterben, a Novelle von Arthur Schnitzler*, a friend of the Freud family and the same man whose revival piece was being performed at the Burg on this very night. One last book, I noticed, was wedged in a corner and was almost concealed under a flap of the cardboard. Upon further inspection, it proved to be a small brown velvet-covered book, decorated with gold-toned metal clasps and hammered leaves. Long-faded handwriting on the cover page said simply, *Diary of Minna Bernays*.

I realized that this must be the same Minna to whom Freud had dedicated his book. Although my knowledge of Freud was fairly broad, I was not familiar with Minna, so I curiously delved further into the little diary.

Three faded photographs were tucked inside the cover. One, dated 1896, with a brownish tint, had probably been illuminated by gaslight. It was of a woman who seemed to be about thirty, with dark brooding eyes, a small tender smile, and a dimpled chin. Long black hair framed her oval face. The next photograph was of the same woman, perhaps a little older and a little heavier, wearing a white high-necked dress with long sleeves puffed at the shoulders. This time her hair was neatly pinned back into a bun and she stood in a formal pose next to a slim, intense-looking bearded man in a black suit— vest, crisp white shirt, and polka-dot bow tie: unmistakably Sigmund Freud. The doctor looked quite serious but with a set to his posture that seemed almost aggressive and a sparkle in his eyes. In her left hand the woman held a book. The year 1899 was scrawled on the back of the photograph, followed by these words: "On the occasion of my book which will disclose the secret of dreams. Sigmund"; and then in Latin, *Flectere si nequeo superos, Acheronta movebo,* which I roughly translated as "If I cannot please Heaven I'll raise Hell."

My heart pounded with excitement as I realized the enormity of my discovery. Almost fearful that it would all be snatched out of my hands, I quickly examined the last photograph. The third find also showed Freud and the woman; this time he was wearing a mountain hiking outfit—knickers banded at the top of high boots and a woolen Tirol coat. The woman, nestled close to him, wore a becoming ankle-length peasant dress and dirndl with a low neckline, giving just a hint of her full figure. Dark hair flowed casually over her shoulders and dress. The two were smiling and relaxed, as if after a pleasant outing. The scene was intense with shadows but the two were bathed in sunlight. The inscription on the photograph was, *Bolzano 1900. Minna and Sigi.*

I settled myself more comfortably, propping up my feet on a small bookcase and leaning my back against a sturdy box. A single light bulb overhead provided just enough light to make out the ornate handwriting in the little book. Entranced, I turned the pages and entered into Minna's life.

# 1895

## November 26, 1895

I am the dreamy sister, the one they call romantic and impractical, compared to my sister Martha. Now the difference between us is more clearly seen for Marty has her own home, children, and husband – while I am merely a guest here at 19 Bergasse, no matter how kindly they welcome me.

For some time now, I have felt that I am without direction. I have been living with Mama for so many years, and since the death of my beloved Ignaz my life has seemed to be without meaning. Although I am only thirty years old, I fear I am turning into a bitter old woman. When Marty asked if I would come to help in her confinement, I could not refuse. And so here I am.

Her sixth baby is due any day now, and with this pregnancy, Marty is more irritable and unhappy than I have ever seen her. I know that she didn't want to conceive again, and it seems almost as if the infant knows it. So poor Martha suffers with great discomfort in her back and abdomen and with a persistent kidney infection, and she is barely able to eat. As she is so petite, the baby seems very large within her.

Although I know that they have financial troubles, their home in Vienna is very impressive. Martha says that Sigmund must keep up a good appearance for the sake of his patients and reputation, but knowing her, I'm sure that she encouraged these comforts for her own pleasure. Marty is like that – always concealing her own desires behind "unselfish" reasons. Mama is like that too.

This is a big stone building with the main apartment on the second floor. Sigmund's study is near the entry. Martha is happy with this arrangement, which gives her little contact with his patients. She says his work must be kept separate from their family life. I wonder if she resents his work? She certainly doesn't seem to be terribly interested in what he is doing.

Every room of the flat is filled with beautiful furniture complemented by pieces of Martha's fine needlework. (Perhaps later I will be able to display some of my work – which, I can modestly say, compares well with hers for skill and perhaps even better for imagination.) They have not yet had electricity installed, although I've been told there are a few electric streetlights in the quarter.

After I exchanged greetings with the family, the housekeeper showed me to my sitting room, just off the family's sitting room, and then to my bedroom. I was a bit surprised and concerned to see that my bedroom connects with Martha's and Sigmund's. What of our privacy since I will have to pass through their room to reach mine? With all the children I suppose they are short of bedrooms. I shall just have to make do with what is available.

## November 27, 1895

I spent most of my first day keeping the children occupied and learning the routine of the household. It was both tiring and exciting, as new things sometimes are. The children are wonderful—so full of life and imagination. Marty has been so miserable and short of temper with them that I know they will welcome my presence. I think we will get along splendidly.

Finally this evening, I had time to talk with Sigmund. We have always been warm with each other and, indeed, he and my Ignaz were close friends. Several times I have loaned him money (of course, without Martha's knowledge; she would be terribly embarrassed). He is appreciative—but beyond that, there is something in us that matches. All day I had so been looking foward to a chance to chat with him.

I sat down with a small pile of mending in the sitting room, just across the hallway from his study door. I took a chair that had a clear view of the doorway so that I would not miss him should he emerge.

At last, as I had almost finished the mending, the study door opened and my brother-in-law slowly entered the hallway. He was so deep in thought that he appeared to be having difficulty properly buttoning his vest. Gradually, he raised his eyes and saw me.

"Why, Minna," he said, his voice hoarse from smoking and silent work but warm all the same, "willkommen to Wien. It is so good you could come to help us." He gave me a friendly kiss on the cheek then walked to a red-leather chair near mine and sat down. The cushion squeaked with his weight and he tossed an embroidered pillow aside as he settled himself comfortably.

"How is Emmeline?" Sigmund asked matter-of-factly.

"Oh, Mother is as always. Still strong-willed and enjoying her friends in Hamburg. She resisted my coming here but finally saw a better possibility of marrying me off from here, I think. You know how she hates Vienna — but slightly less than she hates the thought of me an old maid." I laughed rather nervously, wondering what had prompted my remarks about marrying.

Sigmund smiled and nodded thoughtfully. I know he has not been overly fond of Mama since she decided years ago to move the family from Vienna back to Hamburg just after he and Marty were betrothed. He can't forgive her for causing the five-year separation that eventually forced him to stop his research work with cocaine due to frequent visits with Martha. In some deep way, I think he may blame Mama because another doctor was able to anticipate his findings about the numbing effects of cocaine and publish them before Sigmund could publish his.

"I'm glad I didn't let Mama talk me out of coming," I said, noticing Sigmund's intense dilated eyes looking deeply at me. "The family needed me here, and there is no longer anything for me in Hamburg."

"Yes." Sigmund spoke in a voice so low I had to strain forward to hear. He appeared to be deep in thought again. "Yes, there is more for you in Vienna. Next week there is a Schubert concert I think you will enjoy."

"I am sure I will have plenty of time to experience the culture Vienna has to offer," I said a bit stiffly. Did he think of me simply as a visitor to be entertained? "But for now, let me help in whatever way I can with Martha and the children."

He nodded again. Silence fell between us.

"How is your work?" I asked, searching for a comfortable topic. I felt strangely flustered.

Sigmund leaned back and reached into his vest pocket for a cigar.

"That depends on how you look at it," he said chuckling. "The patients aren't rushing through the door and we aren't getting richer — but Josef Breuer and I are discovering a new method to heal troubled minds."

"Does it involve the use of electricity?" I asked, having read in the newspaper of its use for patients with mental symptoms. I confess I wanted to impress my brother-in-law with my knowledge.

"No, Minna. Nothing like that," Sigmund responded. "Ours we call the cathartic cure. We can cure symptoms caused by emotional distress by bringing back the original feeling of the event that triggered the disturbance."

"Do you mean that something that occurred years ago can still affect a person?" I asked hesitantly.

"An effect!" Sigmund exclaimed enthusiastically. "An effect! The event is like the irritation in the oyster causing the pearl, and we can get to that irritation." He became quieter. "Minna, this work may explain all of the disturbances, the rages, the frenzies, and the fears. There is a common factor." He looked up quizzically, expecting a response.

"Is it heredity?" I ventured. "I don't know that much about psychological theory, but . . ."

"Yes, yes," he said impatiently. "That has been the prevailing theory up until now — that hysteria is constitutional, biologically determined, and without a cure. Professor Baron Richard von Krafft-Ebing pioneered that view, but I have gone deeper, far deeper, and there is a common root." He looked intensely at me for a few seconds and I felt a flush beginning at my throat. Sigmund went on. "At the core of hysteria, the core of neurosis, there is a sexual factor."

"What do you mean?" I asked uncomfortably. He didn't seem to notice my distress and continued, absorbed in what he was saying. "Through the memories, one leading to another, the chains of memory and association lead me back and back to an early sexual trauma. Hours of work with each patient allows the veil to be lifted — in some we must return to earliest childhood, to a childhood seduction."

I was relieved as Martha walked ponderously into the room. She was looking pale and leaned heavily on the back of my chair. "Minna," she said breathlessly, "I am feeling so weak. How my head and back hurt. I don't think I've ever felt so bad. Sigmund, can you spare Minna for a few moments so she can help me?"

I took the opportunity to escape from the unsettling conversation. "Yes, Marty might enjoy a neck rub to relieve the tension. I enjoyed our talk," I said quickly and turned to leave with my sister.

Sigmund called after me. "Minna, we must learn that everything can be studied. *Guten abend.*" So he had perceived my discomfort after all.

Martha had told me in her letters how single-minded Sigmund is. When he is off on a psychic exploration, she said, he can talk or think of little else. I had thought this a rather self-serving comment, knowing that she does not altogether approve of his work, but now I too had experienced his intensity. It would be strange to adjust to living again with such scholarly stimulation.

I peeked in on the children to be sure they were all sleeping soundly on my way to Martha's bedroom. She was waiting on a low bench and moaned with discomfort as I began to run my hands along her neck. I started to think back upon our childhood days, and I remembered most of all the intellectual passion of the Bernays family. At the age of twelve, enthralled by the discussions, I would sit for hours at the intricately carved dining table, with Grandpa Isaac's picture looking down on us from the wall, his official portrait as chief rabbi of Hamburg. There would be Uncle Michael, Uncle Jakob, and my father, Berman, talking, debating, gesturing, making their points. Only once did the conversation erupt into anger and true fury—when Uncle Jakob announced that he was giving up Judaism to be lehr-consul to the king of Bavaria.

After Papa died, the December I was thirteen, we had no more discussions around that table. I used to creep into the dining room to try to recapture the safe feelings Papa had provided but would find only quiet emptiness.

I finished Marty's rub and helped her into bed. She seemed so helpless, like another child to care for.

## November 28, 1895

My poor feet are aching from standing all day. It is late at night and I have taken refuge in my bedroom. I must admit that the children wore me down today. I can't imagine how Martha has been able to manage with them in her present state of fatigue. She seems to be able to keep everything moving smoothly while being pulled in several directions at once. I wonder if Sigmund appreciates the amount of work it takes to keep this busy household running. From what I have seen these last few days, I believe that he is so involved in his work that most of the time he barely notices the family. Maybe on the weekend when he

5

visits his parents, Amalie and Jakob, he will be more fully present.

Sometimes for a moment, when my mind is elsewhere and I catch just a glimpse of Sigmund from the corner of my eye, I imagine he is Ignaz. They were such good friends before Martha and Sigmund were married, and I know that for Sigi, too, the loss was a heavy one, although he did not show it.

One of the very few times I can remember allowing myself to cry was when my beloved Ignaz died. As a child, I was taught never to show my feelings – not even in our own home. Mama said we had to be strong to survive in the world. Ignaz opened me to feelings, to expression; first love, such radiant love, and I thought we would be together forever.

His face is so clear in my mind that I feel as if we had parted only yesterday rather than eight years ago. How can the time have passed so quickly? I see his delicate face, the thin beard he tried so hard to grow so he could look more like the rabbis, his brown eyes that held so much emotion. He was my lover, my first and only, and in the beginning, I felt great shame because of it. I have tried for years now to stop dreaming of him in the daytime; I still dream of him often at night. Ignaz, my beloved Ignaz.

Sigmund once said to me years ago, "We are wild and passionate people in our hearts." I recall not knowing whether it was he and I that he meant or all of humanity. I had just confessed to him that I had loved Ignaz since I was sixteen. In my innocence, I "knew" that we were to be a joyous quartet, Ignaz and myself, Sigi and Martha. I could have continued to live out my happiness then.

My Ignaz could not yet afford a wife, though, and I, wanting to be a dutiful daughter, would not go to England with him. What a fool I was. I could have worked, taught children, while he studied for his degree at Oxford. I will always believe that if we had been together the tuberculosis would not have taken such hold, that the power of our love would have restored his health. By the time he returned, so thin and sick, to seek out Sigmund for medical advice, I knew it was too late for us. His larynx had been affected. There seemed to be no hope any longer for the life we had planned together, and so we broke it off. He broke it off, rather, and I let him.

"I don't want to keep the woman I love bound to a sick and dying man," he had said, his voice weak and raspy. I, young and tied to Mama's apron strings, I let him go. The next month, with what little strength he had left, he climbed to the roof at 18 Mariahilfer Strasse and leaped to his death.

I remember my Uncle Michael saying, "It is God's will." I have sustained myself with such thoughts for all these years—that beloved God would not have taken my Ignaz without reason—and yet, being here, seeing the life and home Sigi and Marty share, my memories and my grief surge back more powerfully than ever.

I will make only one vow to fate: If love again enters my life, I will follow it, I will hold onto it, wherever it leads. My heart, not Mama or fear, will guide me. This time I will be true to myself—no matter what the price.

## November 29, 1895

It is strange to live in a household where there is a man again, and Sigi's presence is especially strong. When he is in one of his melancholy moods, the whole family suffers from it—and we are always reminded of him by the constant odor of cigar smoke. Marty hates the cigars. "These ashes everywhere spoil the house," she says fretfully. "No sooner does our housekeeper make everything clean and tidy than there are ashes everywhere all over again."

Martha seems more like Mama these days: fussy, closed-minded, easily annoyed. After Papa died, when Marty was eighteen, she and I were bonded together from sorrow, but since that time, we have drifted apart and I have found great difficulty in recapturing that closeness.

Even now she has no suspicion that Ignaz and I were intimate. I've always known that even to hint of it would shock her. So she has no idea of what came after—the fear, the pregnancy and then losing the new life growing inside of me, and the infection that followed. I almost died as the fever went on day after day. Mama, of course, said I was paying for my sins, but as I grew sicker and sicker, even she became gentler as she witnessed my pain. Ignaz never knew and Marty was away on a trip visiting with Sigmund's family. When she returned, she knew only that I had been ill. My sister never knew the extent of my grief, the grief of Ignaz's death, and the lasting sorrow that I would never bear any man's child. The infection had left me barren.

In Hamburg, I retreated to solitude and my books and barely left the house. My garden withered. My work with children as a governess during the next few years somehow kept me going, giving me a reason to continue from day to day. Deep within myself, however, I was unsatisfied — always wondering what my life would have been like with my Ignaz and our child.

Martha's letter asking for help seemed to be a chance for a new beginning. Uncle Jakob quoted the Talmud, saying, "If you change your location you can change your life." I hope that living with a family again will remind me that I can be useful and strong.

The children demand a lot of attention, but I am fond of them all. Jean Martin, the oldest boy, named after one of Sigmund's teachers in Paris, a Dr. Jean Martin Charcot, is the child with whom I have most affinity. Mathilde is a sturdy, intelligent girl just as I was at her age, and the three younger children are playful imps. Sigmund says that if the new baby is a boy he will be named Wilhelm, after Sigi's friend, Wilhelm Fliess, and if it is a girl her name will be Anna, named for one of Dr. Breuer's family members. Sigi believes in naming children for a reason. "You call the spirits down with a name," he joked once, "like Faust calling forth Mephistopheles." Oliver was named for Oliver Cromwell, Mathilde is the name of Josef Breuer's wife, Ernst honors Ernst Brucke, one of Sigmund's greatest teachers, and Sophie was named after my aunt who gave Sigi a loan so he could marry Martha.

Marty says she does not care at all about the infant's name or even whether it will be a boy or a girl. She simply wants to be out of her misery.

## December 1, 1895

Six days now and I am feeling more like part of this household. The children have started to accept me so that I can relieve Martha of some of her work. Even the housekeeper has consulted me on a few minor matters, and she does not take kindly to strangers.

Before arriving, I had thought of taking up the piano, but because of the closeness of our bedrooms I will not do so. Sigmund is steadfast in his dislike of musical instruments in the house. He claims that it disturbs his patients, but, as I know, he himself does not really enjoy music.

The cold has begun in earnest now. I go out as little as possible. The older children are bundled from head to toe before leaving for school each morning.

Martha is still unhappy, troubled by the swelling of her hands and feet. She can no longer wear her wedding ring. I certainly hope that the baby arrives soon.

## December 2, 1895

The house today has been dark and gloomy. Marty is extremely uncomfortable and is overdue now by several days. The children are all sick with colds, and Sigmund works long hours in his study even after he is finished with his analytic patients. The practice is slow and he worries about money. I hope that my own small nest egg, which I have given over to him, will help.

Martha's friends come calling regularly every afternoon. For the past few days, though, she has refused to see them, claiming fatigue. She has always had the ability to make and keep many friends, although I think she is not very close to anyone. To my knowledge, she has not stayed in touch with any of her old friends from Hamburg.

Like me, Sigi, too, does not seem to have many close friends. He is closest to Wilhelm Fliess, an ear, nose, and throat doctor in Berlin, and although they rarely see each other, they exchange letters regularly.

Sigmund tells Wilhelm all of his ideas and plans when they meet at "congresses," as they call them. Sigi even sent him proofs of his new book on hysteria. "The final polish," he said with satisfaction, "will come from the best mind in Germany.".

This evening, after the children were in bed, I visited Sigmund in his study. The room was thick with cigar smoke – the cigars that Marty hates so and that I know Sigi has tried to give up several times to stop the palpitations of his heart. Now he has resigned himself.

"I need the cigars to work," he told me. "If I die sooner, so be it. Wilhelm says I'll live to be fifty-one anyway." I believe that comes from a formula of Wilhelm's. Dr. Fliess treated Sigi for his heart palpitations and blamed them on smoking, resulting in a fourteen-month "truce in my battle of cigars," as my brother-in-law called it. "The war is lost," he said to me with a childish grin, lighting yet another cigar.

"Martha asked me to have you call Dr. Fleischman tomorrow. She is worried because the baby has stopped moving." I told Sigmund this as I sat in a chair across from his desk.

He sighed. "I will call Fleischman, but I know that he will say this always happens right before delivery."

"Well, I certainly hope so, for Marty's sake. She is so miserable. I'm not sure she can tolerate many more days of waiting."

Sigmund blew a smoke ring that enveloped the small collection of antique statuettes of Roman and Greek gods and goddesses that covers the top of his large mahogany desk. Through the haze, he resembled the Greek god Zeus, even though he is no taller than I, barely five-foot-seven, and weighs just 135 pounds. Yet, like the god, he has such assurance and intensity.

Martha is always trying to get him to eat more so he will gain weight, although food is not one of Sigmund's great passions. Yesterday, she prepared *gesottenes rindfleisch*, a boiled beef dish, and fresh poppy-seed rolls, but he barely ate, anxious to get back to his work. I can tell that this is difficult for Martha, who is so proud of her cooking.

Tonight, Sigmund and I talked a little longer and then he began to rub wearily at his eyes and to shuffle aimlessly through a stack of papers that sat on the corner of his desk.

I said, "You work like a man possessed."

He laughed and pointed to the gray that had come so early in his beard, saying, "I am impelled to *travailler sans raisoner* – to work without reason." He stood then and looked out his window to the carriages rolling through Bergasse.

"I have gotten hold of something elusive," he said seriously, "the mind and how it holds on to memories and emotions to bring them out later as symptoms. The key of analysis opens the door and unlocks the emotions, and we have a reaction, release, and, finally, a cure. But it is elusive, for the memories are hidden and guarded by the ego, which finds the ideas repugnant and erects a resistance."

Sigmund talks to me as an equal, almost as a colleague, as we sit together in his study, and I feel a part of my intellect that has been unused for some time now begin to stir. I feel so ignorant next to his brilliance and am flattered that he shares his ideas with me. Marty said she never could understand his work, and Sigi appears to have little patience with her. He has said nothing to me about their relationship, but I fear it is strained.

There is something in the way he looks at me that is very much a man looking at a woman. His gaze is not truly improper, yet I feel a sort of energy between us that I have not felt in many years — not since Ignaz and I were together. As his excitement mounts with his ideas, I feel quickened. I listen raptly.

I am surprised to see that Sigmund still keeps cocaine in his office; there is a small bottle of white powder with a needle and syringe next to it. I knew that some years ago he had experimented with it, but after his friend, the promising Ernst Fleishl, became addicted, I thought that Sigi had given it up. He seemed a bit annoyed when I casually mentioned it to him so I have not broached the subject again. Perhaps he thinks he needs it to complete his work. He certainly seems to push himself to a physical extreme.

Occasionally, I feel almost as if my presence here is reliving the days of Marty's and my childhood. Just as she followed Mama around and wanted to be like her, now she *is* the Mama, and just as I used to go with Papa to hear the rabbis discuss the issues of the day, glorying in intellectual challenge and the talk of men, now it is almost the same when Sigmund and I sit together in his study. It makes me wonder about the course of past and present time. How strongly are these tied together, and how many of our life experiences are simply presented time and time again?

## December 3, 1895

Anna Freud was born at 3:15 this afternoon. She weighs six pounds and fourteen ounces. Marty is becoming more comfortable and Sigi is delighted, calling the baby "a complete little woman." For the first time since my arrival, I could feel the bond between Martha and Sigmund. Perhaps this baby will bring them closer again.

I was up late this evening, I think because of the excitement of the birth. I wandered restlessly throughout the flat until I heard sounds from Sigi's study. He too appeared restless and welcomed my company. He told me he is growing worried about anti-Semitism in Vienna; Karl Lueger is running for mayor on a platform that blames many of the poor conditions in Vienna on the Jews. There is talk about segregating schoolchildren. Lueger's forces claim that Jews control the economy.

We talked for hours and at one o'clock in the morning began a game of two-handed tarok. Sigi's deck is an unusual one, court cards illuminated with historical designs. A gift from his mother, Amalie, they had been used for divination. Even now she continues to use tarot for fortune-telling. Sigmund was teasing her earlier in the evening.

"Mama," he had said to her, "this is an age of science, of reason. Put away your cards."

Amalie, small but with a will of iron, had looked at her Sigi, her "goldener," as she calls him, and answered, "The cards foretell a great future for you, and you want me to give them up? Remember the gypsy when you were born?" Then they both had laughed.

Sigi will only admit to liking the tarok because it mimics life, he says, with all its chances and struggles. "The tarot is mystical nonsense," he had said to Amalie passionately. She had smiled but said nothing.

## December 16, 1895

Little Anna is doing well, but Marty is still irritable and fatigued. "I can barely get out of bed," she said today in an unpleasant, whining manner. "My head is pounding and I am still so weak. I don't believe I will ever recover."

These days, Martha doesn't ask how Sigmund's work is progressing. I do not understand her at all. In some ways, I feel I am more like a man than a woman, with passion in my mind as well as in my body.

Yesterday, to get some relief from her constant complaining, I decided to take a long walk and stop at the Café Herzog, on Leopold-gasse. I wore my new cashmere gown that Mama had given me as a present before my departure to Vienna. It is sapphire blue, lined throughout, with a tight-fitting waist and in back a wateau pleat from the yoke. The front is loose with epaulet shoulders, and a wide ruffle is at the hem. I felt quite regal. Even Martha admired it. She said that she is so anxious to regain her figure and wear some of the latest styles, although so far she still has shown little interest in her friends.

There is a fashionable promenade in the streets of Vienna each day between noon and two o'clock. Although I usually am not interested in such affairs, this afternoon I quite enjoyed being greeted by the gentlemen with their little bows. The wind was brisk and the late winter sun provided only thin, watery light, but the ladies proudly displayed their finery, oblivious to the cold. Small groups of people formed on the street corners discussing the happenings of Vienna. Along the sidewalks women vendors were selling lavender and men pushed steaming carts loaded with roasted chestnuts, apples, potatoes, and hazelnuts through the streets. An organ-grinder entertained a crowd of small children and housemaids with his cheerful music. I was fascinated and refreshed by this active street life.

I have been so busy since my arrival in Vienna that I have yet to make new acquaintances here, and I miss my few friends back home. The Freud household seems to be insulated from the outside world, and perhaps this is Sigmund's choice, to protect his work. In any case, I knew that Amalie and her friends read cards at the café in the afternoon, and, looking forward to seeing her again, I made my way there. A feeling that was almost loneliness had overtaken me, so I hurried on.

By the time I reached the café, I was chilled, and with a warm cup of Café mit Schlag in hand, I sat silently by Sigmund's mother in the steamy room, letting the buzz of conversation lull me, until she stirred me with a question.

"Minna, how is your family?" Amalie has always had a special interest in my scholarly uncles, Michael and Jakob, and we spoke of them for a while. Her father, Solomon, who later turned to textiles to earn a living, was once a rabbi, and he had instilled in Amalie the same love of learning that my papa gave to me. I filled her in with the usual news, mentioning a few things that Mama had written in her last letter.

Rereading what I just wrote about Marty, I fear I have been too harsh. I will never bear a child, and she has borne six. I know that her life has not been what she expected when she married Sigmund. However, she has more now than I will ever have.

## December 24, 1895

It is strange for me not to celebrate Hanukkah, but Martha says Sigi dislikes the religious holidays. For the first time since my arrival, I am a bit homesick for Mama's house. We would be lighting the menorah every night of Hanukkah, reciting the blessing together over the candles. I feel very alone tonight.

No gifts are exchanged here either, so I did not mingle with the Christmas shoppers. The shops have been crowded for weeks now and the holiday spirit is high. In the past, I have felt like an outsider, always murmuring "Thank you" to the inevitable greeting of "Merry Christmas" from the shopkeepers, but this year, not keeping either holiday has made me feel quite isolated.

I read in the newspapers today of the emperor's blue fir Christmas tree. It sounds quite grand. Martha said that Jakob Herzl, an acquaintance of Sigi's, trimmed a "Hanukkah tree" every year. We laughed together, although now, in privacy, I must admit that I would enjoy decorating such a tree.

I can see from the garden window that a light snow has begun to fall, covering everything with a powdery coating. The children will play in the snow tomorrow. In the distance, the bell at Saint Stephen's

Cathedral has begun to toll, calling worshipers to Mass. Windows all along our street are filled with flickering candles.

Although the children are sleeping, I will not visit with Sigi. I am fond of his company but do not wish him to see me in such a melancholy mood.

# 1896

## January 2, 1896

I have been in Vienna for more than a month now, and it feels more like my home. Sigmund and I continue our almost nightly games of tarok, unless he is suffering from a migraine headache. Tonight he gave me a small present, an ancient vessel from Egypt in the shape of a sphinx, with full breasts and small wings. Archaeology is one of his passions, for he says his work is like that, an archaeology of the mind. The statue was on his desk and I had admired it. After our game, he said, "The statue is for you. It looks like you."

I was surprised and said the first thing that came to my mind. "But I wish that I were so beautiful." He only laughed and kissed my hand, and I fear I blushed. I felt a strong attraction to Sigmund, which for the first time I recognize as sexual, and it frightens me. I have been without a man for so long, but Sigi is my sister's husband, and, of course, it must not be.

## January 15, 1896

The household has been quiet for the past several weeks. All goes on as usual. I have been reading a lot and have just finished *Daughters of the Rhineland* by Clara Viebig. She shows life as it is in all its tragedy, but for her the consolation is in work. I admire that yet I also felt a kinship with Clara Dallmer, the heroine. In her soul was one great yearning cry for a vast love, a complete love, a sensual experience to sweep her away. Though I try to stifle it, I too feel that yearning.

## February 4, 1896

The household has been in a state of high excitement about the publication of Sigi's new book, which he wrote with Josef Breuer, *Studies in Hysteria*. Today, however, Sigi was in a black mood because the book had received poor notices in the *Deutsche Zeitschrift für Nerveheilkunde*. Adolph von Strumpell called it "confusing and fanciful." That made me so angry! What power a reviewer has to criticize and destroy. Sigi regards all those who do not understand him as enemies, and he was very upset.

His silence at the luncheon table was painful to me; he barely ate but drank several glasses of wine, which is unusual.

Later today, though, he began to cheer up. "I agree with Heinrich Heine, Minna, that one must forgive one's enemies — but not before they've been hanged!" We both laughed. Then this evening we learned that a sympathetic review by Freiherr von Bergner with the title "Surgery of the Soul" had appeared in the *Presse*. Sigi complained that von Bergner isn't a doctor, only a poet, but I could tell that he was pleased. Actually, von Bergner is an esteemed professor who occasionally directs productions at the Imperial Theatre.

Sigi's work is so much a part of him that when it is criticized, it is as if his own person has been attacked. Apparently, Baron von Krafft-Ebing has continually been critical.

"Krafft-Ebing is the leading expert on sexuality," Sigmund explained to me. "He has been since 1886 when his *Psychopathia Sexualis* was published, but he has no interest in anyone else's ideas."

"I saw Krafft-Ebing's name in the newspaper last month," I told him. "He testified in some trial, didn't he?"

"Yes — the forensic expert," Sigmund mocked. "Krafft-Ebing told the court that sexual perversions are constitutional, therefore untreatable. If my theories were acknowledged, they would have rejected his testimony."

"Then there are politics in the world of science too." The realization disturbed me.

"Yes," Sigi replied in a resigned tone. "This is Vienna, where who you know carries you far, and as a Jew, you have no champion."

Still, I can tell that he has great hopes for this new book. The preliminary paper was well received in France by Pierre Janet and in London by Myers and has been translated into Spanish. Josef Breuer contributed cases and insights of his own, and Sigi explained to me the importance of having Josef as coauthor because of his greater experience and prestige. Also, he is a truly devoted friend who has often supported Sigmund with loans of money. Years ago, when I was visiting with Martha and Sigi, Dr. Breuer had told me: "Sigmund's intellect is soaring at its highest. I gaze after him as a hen at a hawk." Then he added, "But I still can't agree with some of his ideas."

Sigmund realizes that the narrow-minded medical circles of Vienna would have condemned his work as too extreme had it not been associated with someone already established, such as Josef, so I was surprised at the vehemence with which he suddenly said tonight, "Josef himself is blinded to the importance of sexual memories in hysteria. I will not write with him again." Like the Hannibal he admires, Sigmund has a battlefield, but his is a battle of minds.

When I read the manuscript of *Studies in Hysteria*, it brought to mind a book Uncle Jakob wrote about Greek drama and the "dramatic catharsis" people experience when they watch great plays on the stage. Sigi was pleased that I saw the relationship between the two books. He told me that he owes some of his ideas to Jakob Bernays but chose not to credit him in the book as my uncle is not a physician.

I found the case histories in the book most fascinating, especially the stories of Anna O. and Fräulein Elisabeth. Anna was only twenty-one, but her symptoms were terrible: problems with her eyes, muscle spasms in her throat so severe she could not eat for three weeks, hallucinations, and loss of hearing and speech. It seemed incredible to me that disturbances of the mind could produce such genuine bodily symptoms, but then I remembered being ill after Papa died and also after Ignaz was buried, and I can imagine that the effects of great shame or great desire might be even more powerful than sorrow. In Anna's case, Dr. Breuer hypnotized her so that she could talk away her symptoms. First, he had rearranged her room so that it resembled her father's sickroom, where she had spent so many hours caring for him as he was dying. By reproducing the scene of trauma, he thought he could help her to rid herself of the dreadful hallucinations born of her fear. Josef devoted days to this patient, and Sigi says it was all Josef could talk about at the time.

The "talking cure" was successful because Sigi told me in confidence that Anna O. is really Bertha Pappenheim, whom I read about just last week in the newspapers! She has become the director of the biggest orphanage in Frankfurt. In spite of her cure, however, she refuses to let any of the women and children in her care undergo "psychoanalysis."

The case of Fräulein Elisabeth confirmed that the "talking cure" works even without hypnosis. Sigmund pressed Elisabeth's forehead to bring out pictures and ideas and learned that she was in love with her sister's husband, but she considered her thoughts too shameful to remember. She felt so wicked for the tender and sensual feelings she had for her brother-in-law that she punished her own body for them with pain.

Reading this case made me uncomfortable, and I self-consciously looked up at Sigi, who was absorbed in writing at his desk. Of course, such affliction could never come to me because I am of a much stronger moral character. Still, it unsettled me to read about feelings such as those that have begun to stir within me. I wondered if Sigi could see into me the way he had into Fräulein Elisabeth.

He continued to write furiously – as if he couldn't capture his thoughts quickly enough. The gaslight threw shadows that were not unkind across his face. It gave him a softer look somehow, making him appear more approachable. My gaze must have disturbed him for he glanced at me and asked, "Did you finish the manuscript?"

"Yes." I paused thoughtfully for a moment, straightening the stack of papers in front of me. "Did Anna O. fall in love with Josef?"

"I don't know," he replied. "Of course, there is an *ubertragung* – a transference – that occurs naturally, projecting onto the figure of the physician ideas and qualities arising from the content of the analysis, that makes him seem to the patient bigger than life."

But she loved him, I thought. To hold back such passion the way I am holding back mine. Oh, if I could release it, lavish him with all my love, give everything to my beloved. I love him. There, I have said it, and I want to weep.

## February 7, 1896

Martin is ill with a throat infection. I hope the other children do not contract the illness. It is such work caring for a sick child. As Martha is still in a weakened state from the pregnancy and birth, I have spent most of the day at his bedside.

## February 9, 1896

I have been having more dreams and thoughts of Sigi. I know it is wrong, but my passion is rising. I cannot help myself.

Last night, I dreamed I was naked with Sigmund. He had crept into my bedroom, cautioning me against making any sound that might wake Martha. There was no spot on my body that he did not kiss with his burning mouth. As we rolled together in my bed, I tantalized him with my fingers and then with my mouth until I awoke shaking and horrified. I know where some of those thoughts had come from. One of Sigi's patients, Robert R., suffers from neurasthenia (nervous exhaustion and fatigue) due to frequent masturbation. Sigmund accepted his collection of pornographic pictures, as Robert did not wish to have access to them, and last night I found them in one of Sigi's desk drawers. I was so ashamed and excited. I saw them for only a few seconds, yet each one has stayed in my mind. In my dream, Sigi and I were the man and woman in the pictures.

I had hoped that thinking about this again would act as a "talking cure" for myself, but I am afraid I may have made my fantasies worse. I am paralyzed by fear: fear that Marty will know, fear that Sigi will find out, and a great fearful fantasy that he knows already and wants me. Perhaps my fear that he does *not* want me is greater still.

## February 14, 1896

Now Mathilde and Martin are both miserable with throat infections. Sigmund, too, has been suffering with frequent migraine headaches. I certainly hope my good health continues.

## February 16, 1896

For a full week I have prayed for these frightening thoughts to leave my mind, but still they stay. I can no longer sit and talk naturally with Sigi in his study as I once did. I cannot trust what I might do, and so I stay away.

"I am puzzled," he queried me. "What is wrong? I miss your company in the evenings." I could only stutter that the children needed me. My thoughts of him are incessant during the day, and when I lie down they come even more strongly. There are pulsating sensations throughout my body. The devil is tormenting me. God help me.

I try to keep busy with crochet or needlepoint. Even the petit point, the close work one must do to put two hundred silk stitches in each centimeter, can barely divert my mind and aching head from these fantasies. Trying to escape by reading my favorite author, Theodor Fontane, my thoughts fly from the words. It is fate! The book is the story of Effi Briest, an adulteress, punished dearly for her sins by being expelled from her home and dying alone in London.

My only hope is to leave Vienna. I must find a governess post elsewhere. Even more than the shame I feel is the pleasure. I am happy just being in the same house with Sigmund. Obsessed! My love has taken away my power to think, to read, even to reason, and yet there is a part of me that craves these sensuous feelings, this overpowering desire for a man. I can think of nothing more painful than to leave this house and the man I love – and yet I must.

## February 18, 1896

I received a confirmatory letter from a family in Frankfurt about my acceptance of the governess position. It must be — I cannot continue here.

## February 19, 1896

This morning, I entered Sigi's office after knocking briefly. Apparently I startled him, for he shuffled the paper he had been writing on under a stack of books.

"We must meet outside," I said to Sigmund, "I need to speak with you."

He looked up at me, surprised by the urgency in my voice. "What is this about, Minna? Let us discuss it here, in privacy."

I shook my head, speechless and blinded by tears.

"If it is important I can make time to meet you," he said in a concerned way. "Perhaps the Ronacher Café on Alsterstrasse. But why the mystery? Can't we talk here as we always have?"

"Please. I can't," I whispered. "I will meet you at three o'clock — the Ronacher."

I walked in the cool cloudy afternoon across the new tram tracks, so lost in my thoughts that a *fiacre* driver shouted "Stupid woman!" as he veered his horse sharply. Oblivious to the world while waiting in the café, I was startled when Sigi sat down across from me.

"Minna, here I am. Let us talk."

"I must leave Vienna immediately. I have accepted a post in Frankfurt." I just blurted it out, unable to say it in a gentler way, and Sigmund looked shocked.

He almost stammered his reply. "Is there something I have done or said to offend you?"

"I feel I must go. It is a personal matter." I was finding it difficult to breathe in the steamy warmth of the café.

"But Marty and the children need you," he said softly, "and I, too, need your help."

"My help? But how can I help you?" I tried to control my rising emotions. "I know nothing of your work."

"You can begin by helping with translations, and Minna, you alone, of all the women I know, have an understanding of my work." His expression was so loving and concerned that my heart pounded and perspiration dewed on my forehead. I cannot confess, I thought. He must not know.

I have become very aware of the distance between Sigi and Marty. I am sure their marital relationship is not what it once was, and these thoughts of unfulfilled needs have created a dangerous excitement in my mind. Last night, I dreamed of poisoning Martha, and the dream was so vivid. I saw myself putting a white powder into her afternoon tea, and I knew then that I could marry Sigmund. In the dream, I felt a great relief. When I awoke, I was sickened.

"Sigmund," I said finally, "I have been having dreams of horrible things." I could not tell him more. I tried to get up and leave but found myself weak and shaking.

Sigi took my hand and pulled me back to my chair. "Tell me about them," he said gently, but I shook my head. His eyes bored into me with an intensity I found frightening. "Minna," he said after a moment of tense silence, "we need to be honest with each other. Not only can you help Marty with the tasks of the household and with the children but you can help me as well. You do." He paused and sipped his coffee. "I need you, Minna, for my work. You bring a freshness to my mind that I had forgotten. You know that your education has been wasted until now, and I can help you develop your mind."

His phrase "I need you" echoed in my head over and over. The last time I had heard that was from my beloved Ignaz. Is it possible that I was being offered a way to erase the guilt I had carried for so many years?

"I don't know. It is all so complicated," I managed to say, tears running down my face. I tried to hide myself behind the white linen napkin to avoid the curious looks from a man sitting at the next table.

"Minna, my dear," Sigmund said, first squeezing my fingers and then raising them to his lips for a soft kiss.

I looked deeply into his eyes, finding the remedy for all my fears. I whispered, "I will stay." God forgive me, for now I know I cannot turn back.

## February 28, 1896

I accompanied Sigmund this evening on a long walk. As we strolled along, I noticed the emperor's yellow shields, posted at the courthouse and the railroad station, emblazoned with a double-headed black eagle. Occasionally, we glimpsed an Austro-Hungarian officer in his blue or green tunic and white trousers. Sigmund muttered under his breath that they were like the plumage of the parakeet. This made me smile for quite a while and many a gentleman tipped his hat to me, thinking the smile was for him.

We walked mostly in silence. Of late, I have been keeping a distance from Sigi. I feel this is best. I am so confused about my feelings for him, desiring him as a man and yet knowing that he is my sister's husband. The attraction I feel is so strong, and I think, or at least I hope, that he, too, is attracted to me. I must maintain my composure. This is the path I have chosen.

## March 20, 1896

Tonight, during our tarok game, Sigmund began telling me about his relationship with Marty. We were settled quite comfortably, having pulled a small table and chairs up close to the ceramic coal stove to ward off the late-night chill.

"Martha is a fine woman, Minna," he said, speaking slowly. "When I first met her, she was so lovely, so fresh and innocent. I'm afraid I have not made marriage easy for her. She loves the children, but they came so quickly and they demand so much that somehow the two of us have grown apart."

Nervously, I twisted a tassel on a pillow from my chair, wanting to hear and yet not wanting to. It was a dangerous moment, for I knew such knowledge would only fuel my passion. Sigmund seemed to need so much to speak, however, that I had to let him go on.

"Since Anna's birth, she has been terrified of conceiving again." I saw the torment on his face as he said this. "Perhaps I expect too much from her."

The pounding in my head increased until I could no longer sit still. My heart ached to comfort him, and yet I knew I couldn't. What could I say? Pleading fatigue, I soon excused myself and returned quickly to my room. I leaned against the cold bedroom door and closed my eyes. Oh, Sigi. I too am a woman. Why can't it be?

## April 11, 1896

Much must be done to prepare the family for the wedding of Sigmund's sister, Rosa. Marty has not yet fully recovered from the birth and still has very little strength, requiring me to take over the necessary tasks.

This afternoon, I inspected the children's best clothing. Except for a small tear to be mended in Mathilde's white frock, all appeared to be in order. Little Anna will look so adorable in Sophie's pink velvet. It is lucky she was a girl – the boys' handed-down clothing is usually in sad repair.

Tomorrow morning, I must speak to Marty about her appearance. Perhaps she will let me dress her hair for the occasion. It would not do for her fatigue to be obvious to the guests. Sigmund would be quite upset. He has discovered my love of jokes. He even suggested collecting them for a book. I do not know if this is wise. It would mean spending more time together – alone. Just the thought of being with him, even in that way, makes me tremble. I am afraid that I cannot trust myself any longer.

## April 15, 1896

This afternoon, I found Martha in the kitchen polishing the Sabbath candlesticks. It is a task she never trusts to the housekeeper. "The Lord expects it of us. It is a small thing to offer," she always says when Sigmund chides her. The shadows under her dark eyes were heavier today.

"Martha, at least let me do that for you," I offered, putting my arm around her shoulders. "You look so tired."

"Oh, Minna. You are such a help. I had a terrible night. All night long I tossed and turned. I don't know what is wrong with me. Nothing seems to help." She sighed and brushed at her hair with the back of her hand, tucking in a few loose strands. "I have turned into a tired old woman — while you have such energy. Thank goodness Sigmund has taken to you. It relieves me of a great deal of tension."

"Marty, I had no idea you were so upset." I took the silver cloth from her and began polishing, glad for something to occupy my hands. She slumped back in her chair and stared out the window at the children playing in the garden.

"These days I remind myself of Mama, always so full of criticism. I wonder why she was always so unhappy. At least Papa loved her." The tears in her eyes made my throat ache. In all of our years growing up together, I never had seen Marty cry.

Guilt welled up in me once more. Here was the sister that I envied, with her fine home and lovely family, yet she was so unhappy. How could I do anything to hurt her more? I struggled to find something comforting to say. "Marty, you know that Sigmund loves you. He is so proud of you and the children." I could think of nothing more to add.

She gave me a small smile. "You are such a comfort. I meant what I said, you know. You give Sigmund the companionship that I have not been able to give him for years now. He is so much more content now that you are here, and if he is content, the rest of us can be happy." Just then outside Martin fell down and began to cry loudly. I started to rise but Marty motioned me to stay. "Please," she said. "You can do more good here finishing the candlesticks for me. Maybe some fresh air will ease my headache."

My mind and heart are so confused. I don't know if I should rejoice for Martha's blessing of our intellectual relationship or be filled with guilt. I will pray tonight when the candles are lit. Perhaps God will help me.

## April 28, 1896

Annerl's first tooth appeared today. She is growing so quickly!

This afternoon, Martha and I visited with Jakob and Amalie to complete the last-minute wedding preparations. Marty was tired and would not have gone if Sigmund hadn't insisted. She was angry and sulked in the carriage until we arrived, then she became a different person, controlled and friendly. I wondered how many times before she had made herself put on this act.

Jakob and Amalie's house overflows with pictures and mementos of the past. Looking at them, I marveled that so much could happen in a lifetime. Each dish, every statue (mostly gifts from Sigmund), and each little figurine has its own story. Amalie has a fine touch with houseplants, too, and on every available surface there is some variety of plant growing lushly, blooming with bright flowers.

The furniture is a bit worn but very comfortable. Amalie keeps the house spotless – and that seems to annoy Sigmund when he visits as she forever fusses at him about his cigar ash. While Marty and Amalie were in the kitchen preparing coffee, Jakob and I began reminiscing about the old times. Weddings bring back so many memories. I asked how he and Amalie had come to marry.

"I was still grieving over the death of my second wife, Rebekah, when I met Amalie Nathanson. I was attracted to her, a dreamy, romantic girl with a core of ambition and strength. She saw my faults as virtues, my age as wisdom, my two grown children as proof of my experience." He chuckled and shook his head in fond remembrance.

"Her family had little money, you know, after her father's death, and I was able to offer Amalie a more secure life when we married. The textile business was going well, even expanding, but then it was decided that the Northern Railway, which had been planned to pass through Freiburg, would go through a neighboring hamlet instead – a handsome bribe from the mayor of that town had changed the deal. As a result, my business suffered; in fact, all the businesses in town suffered, but I decided to stay in Freiburg and see what would happen. Hard times, easier times, marriages, children, even the deaths of people I loved dearly – all this is part of life. As I grew older, I grew more and more accepting of the ups and downs, and Amalie respected, I believe even needed, my equanimity, and this brought out my paternal nature." Jakob's voice had grown soft and I realized he had forgotten I was there. He was speaking to himself, remembering their early life together.

"But after a time, Amalie wanted to move on, to search for better opportunities and a better education for little Sigi," he continued. "By the time we moved to Vienna, it was clear that money would remain a problem. I became more and more immersed in studying some Hebrew religious works, and soon we needed a loan to help us. My father, Schlomo Sigmund, had better business sense than I, but he died a few months before Sigmund was born. I don't know. Some people are better than others at such things. Sigmund, with his dark spells, would never have made a good businessman, but his brother, Alexander, does well with his imports and exports. My own path is that of a thinker. If it wasn't for Amalie's drive, I would have concentrated on studying Kabbalah, to the exclusion of everything else. God takes care of those who do his works, but I wanted to please my wife.

"Sigmund's bent toward medicine delighted Amalie. To her mind, being a doctor was the most secure profession. For myself, though, that kind of responsibility would have seemed too great. Since I never hungered for fame or great discoveries, Amalie diverted her ambitions to Sigmund. You know that he lived with us here until he was twenty-eight?

"When Sigmund asked my advice, which wasn't often, I always told him that he must follow his inner calling. His mother liked to read the tarot, calling it a kind of spiritual communication. Personally, I always prayed directly to God and then looked in my life and in the Torah for answers."

Marty and Amalie came into the room bearing a tray of coffee and *Kaffee Kuchlein*. The precious moment was broken. "I have always been proud of Sigmund," Jakob added quickly. "I only wish he had more time for me," he said quietly in a quavering voice.

"Oh, Jakob," Marty said, rushing to embrace him, "you know how much we all love you. Sigmund is just very busy with his work. It is even hard for him to find time with me these days."

"Now here is a fine woman," Jakob said, his eyes twinkling. "She often comes to visit this old man. I just wish she wasn't so worn out by all those children. Minna, you must see that she doesn't overtire herself."

"I'm sure Minna has been an enormous help since her arrival," Amalie said, pouring the coffee. "Oh my. We forgot the sugar, Martha. Excuse me, I'll be right back." She hurried back to the kitchen.

Jakob gazed fondly after her. "Amalie has been a fine and devoted wife, but now she has her own life and many lively friends. It seems the difference in our ages is catching up with us. My heart is weakening, and sometimes I wake in the middle of the night suffocating, hearing gurgling sounds in my lungs. I do not fear death, but I am not the man I was." Marty and I exchanged glances. "I have found peace and my life is full—three wives, two families, wonderful children scattered all over, and grandchildren — yes, it has been fruitful and my seed has spread."

"I hope you aren't being depressing," Amalie chided, returning with the sugar bowl. "You still have many years left on this earth." She caressed his shoulder lovingly. "Minna, Martha has told me how much you have been helping Sigmund with his work. I am so happy that he has been able to continue to be productive. He has such a difficult time overcoming the obstacles his colleagues put in his way." I blushed and wondered if my torrid emotions were visible to any of them. "Sigmund's work is very important to me. I just hope I can be of help." Such a shallow answer, but it seemed to satisfy them. No one, *no one*, must know of the passion raging within me.

## April 29, 1896

Listening to Sigi has stimulated areas in my mind that I never knew existed. My thoughts churn and come together. Many nights, they so excite me that I am unable to sleep.

While I was in the nursery this evening, putting the children to bed, I realized how sexuality is with us from childhood. They suck on bottles or thumbs, we pat their backs to put them to sleep, hold and rock them in warm embraces. Children are sexual beings. I must tell Sigi of my thoughts in the morning. Perhaps he will find the idea interesting.

## May 1, 1896

"You cannot begin to guess what a relief it is to me that Rosa has finally gotten married!" Amalie gushed, taking me aside.

"I see you've had a lot of wine. You're sparkling almost as much as the champagne in your glass," I said, teasing her. I was not in the mood for a conversation about marriage.

It was the kind of affair Amalie loves. Mathilde and Sophie had hung yellow daisy chains all over our normally somber salon, and vases were arrayed on tables and shelves everywhere, filled with creamy white lily-of-the-valley bouquets. A little group of musicians was playing, and strains of a waltz filled the air. Sopherl looked lovely in her wreathed crown of forget-me-nots.

"You're right," Amalie said with a smile, "and if Rosa had married sooner, we would not be having this party today!" She twirled her black-and-red-fringed gypsy skirt girlishly. "I adore being the mother of the bride – so I can do all the arranging."

I agreed with her that the French champagne, the music, the laughter, and the family filling the room were fine. Tonight even Marty seemed to sparkle. She looked so happy holding little Anna and chatting with the guests. I realized that this was what she was best at – her public appearance could not be faulted. Sigi was wise to choose her for his wife. He needed all of Martha's tact and social grace to help him further his career. A twinge of jealousy ran through me. These are things I would never be able to provide for Sigmund.

"Rosa looks so beautiful! I can't imagine why she waited so long," Amalie continued.

"She was waiting for the right man. After the spat with Brust, she wanted to be careful," I ventured. "She is a romantic. She needed to feel her heart stolen away from her."

"Careful," Amalie said, snorting. "Careful! Rosa is thirty-six years old. How careful can you be?"

"I am over thirty now, and what is your suggestion for me?" I asked chidingly – but somehow really wanting to know.

Amalie grew more thoughtful. "Minna," she said, "yours is quite another circumstance. You have assumed certain responsibilities, committed yourself to filling certain needs, and you *are* needed here. It is another situation entirely."

Her voice was softer but her gaze was not. A moment before, Amalie had been gay, flirtatious, slightly drunken; but she could change expression more quickly than anyone I had ever seen. "Do not belittle what your life is now," she continued. "Remember the saying, 'behind every great man stands a great woman.'"

"You are very cryptic," I said, and again her mood changed.

32

"A toast! A toast!" she suggested, filling my empty glass with some wine from hers. "This is my favorite, passed down from a Viennese nobleman far back in the Ferstel family. To astonishing fortune."

"To astonishing fortune," I murmured after her.

Sigi came up to us, smiling. The pink carnation in his buttonhole had slipped out partway, his usually neat hair was rumpled, and he looked more relaxed than he had in weeks. "My two wallflowers, sitting alone on a couch talking while the band is still playing," he chided. "Mama, come dance. Minna, you are next."

"After all, it is Rosa's wedding, and I had feared such an event would never take place," Amalie agreed sweetly.

Until Sigmund returned to claim me for the dance, I daydreamed, watching Rosa with her Heinrich. She had always been the beauty of the family, and today she was radiant. With her face flushed and her long dark shining hair, she looked more like a young girl than a woman in her thirties. Heinrich Graf is intelligent, cultured, and has a rapidly growing law practice, but it was not those things that had transformed Rosa. It fascinated me to watch the process of "falling in love," as it took over people I am close to; I knew it as a kind of madness, but a splendid madness. I did not envy Rosa her love, for I knew it could be no greater than mine, but I did envy the openness, the ceremony she was allowed to create.

Sigi's hand on my shoulder startled me, and I felt an involuntary tremor pass through my body as I looked up at him.

"Our turn now," he said, pulling me up and onto the dance floor.

As we danced, we maintained a respectable distance between us, our fingertips only grazing at each other's elbows. Amalie's wine had enlivened me and my breath came quickly. When Sigi's eyes met mine, they seemed to burn into my soul. We both quickly looked away, and I hastened to find some neutral topic of conversation.

"Are you feeling prepared for your lecture on hysteria tomorrow?"

He seemed to have to make an effort to reply. "Yes, I am not too worried. Of course, there are enemies of my theories in the society, but my presentation will be so strong I am confident I will sway them. I only hope Baron von Krafft-Ebing is not offended."

"Many of your theories contradict his, don't they?" I asked.

"Yes, very much so, but his book was published more than ten years ago, and certainly a physician should be able to accept newer findings in his field."

We waltzed on in silence for a few minutes.

"My worry tonight is my father," Sigi said suddenly as the music ended.

We both looked to the big easy chair where Jakob was sitting, his body slumped down into the cushions. His eyes were closed and his head nodded forward in sleep. "He can barely remember the day's events," Sigi went on in a low voice, "but his memory remains excellent for the happenings of ten or twenty years ago. Older memories seem to be stored in a different part of the brain. I suppose I am always a scientist, even when it comes to my own father," he added ruefully.

"Your scientific mind does not seem to have endangered your tenderness," I said. "Perhaps Jakob could attend your lecture tomorrow? He is so pleased by your accomplishments, I think it would make him very proud."

"Unfortunately, the lecture is only for members of the Society of Psychiatry and Neurology, and I suspect Jakob wouldn't understand a word of it anyway. You are right, though — such things do please him."

We walked together to Jakob's chair and I rested my hand on his shoulder. "Are you enjoying the wedding party, Grandpa Jakob?"

His answering smile was wan. "Yes, indeed. If I didn't have my wonderful Amalie I'd probably be getting married again, just like Rosa. It's a wonderful state, marriage."

"Come now, Jakob. Would you really want to put another lady through such trials and tribulations?" I asked, laughing.

"No bed of roses is without its thorns, but if I were a younger fellow, I might even have my eyes set on you, Minna."

"I can run very fast, Jakob."

"Never too fast to be caught by the right man — or by the man you want. If you wanted, you could have a whole flock of suitors at your door, but you don't want any, do you?"

Sigmund looked uncomfortable, trying to appear involved in conversation with Rosa, who had come to join us, but he was listening intently to our conversation.

"I wouldn't say that, Jakob. I'm just very choosy. Living with a good man is hard enough. Imagine life with a tyrant!"

"Who is the man for you, Minna?" Jakob asked softly. At this, Sigmund quickly moved away from us. I tried not to follow after him with my eyes.

"Well, he would have to be intelligent. You know I couldn't put up for long with a dullard, and while looks aren't everything, I might care for a strong, attractive, dark man – with a beard just like yours." I tweaked his long gray beard and straightened his collar.

"Yes," Jakob laughed, and then he began to cough. "Well, perhaps I could find you such a man nearby."

"But where could you find another man with your charm, Jakob? It might be harder than you know."

He fell silent, still smiling. After a few minutes, I said, "Have you heard Sigmund's good news yet?"

"More good news?"

"Yes. Sigmund has been invited to be the guest speaker at one of the societies of doctors, even though some reviewers did not appreciate the book on hysteria. This honor truly shows that his colleagues respect his work."

"Then Sigi's fortune is improving. It is good to be honored, but it's more important to be happy in what you do. If you are following the path God has intended for you, the rest will come," Jakob said.

"The effects of such a public honor are bound to be felt in his practice, and most likely when the selection for Professor Extraordinarius next takes place, Sigi will be on the list. After an honor like this, who could refuse him?" I looked to Jakob for agreement, but he had nodded off again.

It was very late when the last of the guests had left. For once, the children put up no fuss about going to bed. Marty was clearly exhausted by the day's events, but she seemed unusually peaceful. She embraced Sigi and whispered, "Do you remember? I hope they are as happy as we have been." I was unable to stay in the room – choking with violent emotions. As tired as I was, sleep would not come. I was tormented by visions of Rosa and Heinrich dancing, holding each other. I pulled my dressing gown about me and slipped quietly into the salon where the party had taken place. In the darkness, the daisy chains resembled spiderwebs. Why couldn't this happiness be mine? I have loved twice in my lifetime. My first love died, and the second is forbidden.

Sigmund entered quietly into the room. For a moment, I wasn't sure he had seen me, but then he moved toward me and with his hand gently brushed a tear off my face.

"My Minna," he said. "I cannot offer you such happiness." Then he kissed me, pressing his mouth firmly against mine, our bodies close together. All too quickly he left, as silently as he had appeared. I wonder now if it was a dream.

## May 2, 1896

This morning at the breakfast table, the children were still chattering about Sunday's wedding. "Tante Minna, would you curl my hair like that every week?" Sophie pleaded. Martin wanted a pair of big boots like the ones Heinrich wore when he crushed the ceremonial wineglass. "But why smash the pretty glass?" Mathilde wondered.

"Custom, silly. To bring the couple luck," Martin explained.

"When I grow up, I'm going to be a music man and play a big gold instrument like they did in the band," Oliver announced.

"Me too! Me too! Can I play too?" Ernst piped up, and Anna, the baby, chortled.

Sigi came into the room, apparently in a good mood. "And how is all my rabble this morning?" To Marty and me, he confessed, "Well, I am prepared as much as I will ever be. My lecture tonight should make clear the absolute importance of early sexuality in the development of hysteria. Now recognition of this theory, this truth, rests in the hands of my colleagues."

"You are deserving of this honor," I said proudly, blushing as I thought of our moment last night.

"Thank you, Minna," Sigmund responded without hesitation. Had that kiss been just a fantasy? "But I can't understand why I have been chosen, especially by Krafft-Ebing."

"Krafft-Ebing is the chairman of psychiatry," Martha interjected. "Who is in a better position to assess and understand your work?"

Pensively, Sigmund replied, "Krafft-Ebing and I have our differences, but this provides an opportunity for me to give my proof."

"Are all the case reports in order?" I asked, having helped to compile them over the past weeks.

"All eighteen, and I have been reviewing my presentation to build up to the surprise. All have the common factor—early sexual trauma—but equally important is to give my colleagues the method I use, Breuer's cathartic method, which helped me to discover the truth." He smiled radiantly at us. "This means a lot to our family. The referrals will come from every corner of Vienna. You will see."

"Oh, Sigi, I'm so happy for you," Marty and I exclaimed together, in almost the same words. We smiled at each other foolishly. She reached out and gave me a sisterly hug, then Sigi joined in and the three of us embraced for a moment until the children clamored to join in. Anna, feeling deserted in her high chair, began to cry.

"It's wonderful when Sigi's work is going well, isn't it?" Marty said later as we prepared *rindfleisch*, Sigmund's favorite lunch. "It's difficult not knowing when he will be despairing and when he will be confident that he can part oceans."

"Many great geniuses have been moody," I said, perhaps too defensively.

"Oh, yes," Marty laughed. "Despite my complaining, I know Sigi is a wonderful man. I hope sometime soon you will find as fine a husband for yourself. I saw you watching Rosa and Heinrich at the wedding, but you didn't even try to catch the bridal bouquet to be next in line!"

I shrugged, irritated with the constant talk about marriage. "I haven't anyone in mind."

"Well," she sighed, folding her arms in a way that reminded me of Mama, "I know that you could never marry unless it was truly a love match. Remember the fable Mama read us when we were little, about the two princesses? One said that if she had to choose, she would choose marriage without love . . ."

". . . and the other chose love without marriage," I quickly added, "and you were the first and I the second, but you've been so lucky, Marty.

You seem to have gotten both."

"Lucky? Me?" Marty stopped snipping the ends off the string beans to look at me in surprise. "I suppose I am, although I've always envied you, Minna. I guess I was jealous that you could even answer that question the way you did. You always seemed so free."

We worked in silence for a moment until she mused aloud, "Freedom, loneliness, loneliness, freedom. Are they the same?"

"No!" I startled myself with my vehemence. "The real freedom is in love. In giving yourself over to love. It must be, Marty." In spite of myself, my emotions began to rise.

Marty smiled at me sadly and tilted her chopping board covered with beans over the big steaming bowl. "But Minna, you are still such a romantic. Perhaps freedom may come with love in the beginning, but there is no freedom in having children and, after all, children come with love.

"Do you remember when you were little you wanted to be a rabbi, Minna? You didn't understand when Papa tried to tell you that women couldn't be rabbis. 'But I'll wear pants!' you kept saying. Then you found out that no matter what you wore, you would always be a woman, and there were some things that women just couldn't do. How bitter you were! You stormed around the house trying to get somebody to cut off all your hair, asking the maid . . ."

"It's the first time I can remember Papa ever saying 'no' to me," I interrupted, laughing.

"But thinking love means freedom is the same as thinking a woman who wears pants can be a rabbi. It's a lot harder than that."

"Marty, five minutes ago you were asking me why I didn't catch the bouquet yesterday. Now it sounds like you're trying to talk me out of some marriage I haven't even found!"

"I know, I know," Martha said, sighing. "I guess it's just that I'm so tired. The wedding was beautiful, though, wasn't it? It reminded me of how happy Sigi and I were in our early days together. It seemed as if as long as we were together, anything in the world was possible. I didn't believe there could be hard times, but it's been nine years now and of course we couldn't stay that starry-eyed forever. Passion like that can't last. Oh, don't look at me like that," Marty said, for I must have given her an odd glance.

"Sigi and I are still very happy together. I think we complement each other well. When I am tired, or ill, as when I was carrying Anna, he became a father to me, very gentle and not demanding, and when he is in his black moods, I mother him, soothe him. As I've said before, I'm glad to see you two becoming friends, Minna. Your intellect is better suited to his than mine ever was. In many ways, I admire your reluctance to marry. A friend binds a woman so much less than a husband does."

## May 3, 1896

Martha and I were mending the children's play clothing in my sitting room last night when Sigi came home after delivering his lecture. Although his study is at the front of the flat, we heard the solid walnut door slam resoundingly all the way to the back in my sitting room.

Martha and I looked at each other in silence for a moment. Then, "Go to him, Minna," she said in a tired voice. "I do not know how to comfort him when he is so disappointed. So often I cannot understand him or his work. Perhaps he will listen to you." As she spoke, she folded the trousers she had been stitching and placed them atop a pile of clothing on the table. "It is late now. I think I will retire." Sighing sadly, she rose from her chair. From the doorway, she said softly while shaking her head in wonder, "He always has such high hopes. Such a brilliant man. Help him if you can."

I sat for a moment, staring at the glowing embers in the coal stove, then I walked hesitantly down the hallway to the closed study door and softly knocked. There was no answer. I turned the brass knob of the door and opened it a crack, looking in.

"Sigmund?" He was sitting in a dark corner facing the window. One elbow was propped on the arm of the chair, and his hand covered his eyes. A small light burned, leaving the room in semidarkness. I walked in quietly, shutting the door behind me. Unsure of what to say, I stood behind him and placed my hand gently on his shoulder.

After a moment, he spoke. "It was staged, Minna. Wilhelm said it was set up to discredit my work." His voice was low and hoarse. "I cannot believe Krafft-Ebing would have acted with such overt malice. He called my work a 'scientific fairy tale.' In a public meeting of physicians!

I am ruined."

I began to knead the taut muscles of his neck, noticing with compassion the gray that was beginning to show in his dark, thick hair. "Tell me what happened," I said soothingly in the voice I use with the children. Inside, I was boiling with anger.

"I know he has disagreed with my ideas, yet to have carried out such a dastardly plan! He is certainly aware of the time and financial loss the preparation of this lecture has cost me. You know I had eighteen carefully compiled cases to illustrate my points. I took such pains, anticipating that, at the very least, my findings would be accepted as helpful contributions to science. But perhaps I should have suspected something like this. Krafft-Ebing's article in *Zeitschrift fur Hypnotismus*, stating that he had 'tried the Breuer-Freud method without success,' was a hint." Sigmund sighed heavily and shook his bowed head.

"There was an ominous murmuring in the hall when I said that at the bottom of every case of hysteria will be found one or more cases of premature sexual experience, and then the handclapping at the end was lukewarm, but I had expected to face a challenge. I was prepared to illustrate, point by point, how I had carefully researched, observed, analyzed, and arrived at my findings.

"Oh, Minna. You know the many hours I spent with my patients – giving each time to follow associations and images back to earliest memories – and my attentive listening, traveling with them, awaiting illumination. This method is the means of verification, but they will never try it."

Sigmund went on like this for hours, repeating fragments of his lecture, going over and over all the details of the disastrous evening. It seemed as if he still could not believe what had happened. He said bitterly that one of the physicians had called his work witchcraft. I spoke very little but slowly he began to relax. When finally we parted for the night, he was able to look at me. "I am thankful you are here," he said as we embraced.

I felt closer to him at that time than I have to any other person in my life. Finally, we have reached a point of sharing that no one can ever destroy.

## May 4, 1896

There has been a good deal of tension since the lecture. Martin came home from school yesterday and asked Sigmund tearfully, "Is it true that you are the sex doctor and you ask little girls about sex?" This morning someone passed Martha on the street and hissed "Frau Sex Doctor" after her. Sigmund has said very little since that night. He feels he is ruined and has ruined his family in the process. "Disturbing the sleep of the world," he said, "and now we must pay."

This evening, we had a short conversation in his study. He did not have the heart for our tarok game.

"The violent reaction of the forces of repression only proves my theories. In fact, if sexuality were not so crucial a factor in shaping human beings, why would its mention arouse such an extreme response? My enemies act like threatened men, and yet an empty waiting room will be a heavy price to pay for revealing this truth," he said bleakly.

"Hardest of all for me is the toll this has taken on the family. When my father asked me how the lecture had gone, saying that he hoped it meant 'more respect and financial success,' I did not know how to respond. I finally mumbled that it had not gone well, and he seemed to understand, for he asked no further. I couldn't let him know that henceforth I would be barred from the brain research laboratory and that many of my colleagues have sent messages that they would no longer be referring patients to me. Even Breuer, yes, Minna, my good friend Breuer, hissed at me at the lecture, 'I don't believe a word of it.' This friendship, one of my closest for so many years, is lost. At least Wilhelm supports me still. Dear Wilhelm gives me faith to go on."

"Sigmund, you must not let it drive you to such despair," I said, trying to sound more confident than I felt, even though I believe in him with all my heart. "You know you are right. You know the saying about casting pearls before the swine. Waste no more energy on lectures to those narrow-minded people. We will survive without the money, and there will be a time of revenge. Hannibal was great not because he followed his angry impulses but because he planned his attacks and counterattacks with cunning and daring. I will help you. They have not heard the last of Sigmund Freud!" My heart was pounding as I said this, and I knew it to be true. I vowed to myself that I will not allow his work to be ruined, and although I did not say this aloud, in that moment we were as one. Without his work, neither of us would exist.

## May 29, 1896

Sigmund's stepbrother, Emmanuel, has been visiting this week, and Sigi has taken to talking with him late at night instead of with me. I must not be jealous for I have no claim upon him.

## May 31, 1896

Sigi has been working as hard as ever in spite of his being considered little more than an outcast among his colleagues. Some of his patients have stopped coming, and I can see how this hurts him. Almost no one seeks out his advice now, but he continues to work late into the night. "I must prove them wrong!" he tells us. On Thursday, we stayed up late together in his study, and he went over again and again the links binding neurosis to sexuality.

Sometimes it seemed as if he was talking more to himself than to me. I wanted so badly to help him, to give him strength. When I had first arrived here, I found almost overpowering the artifacts and statutes with which he surrounds himself in his study, but now I have come to realize that, in some mysterious way, they are Sigmund, representing every facet of his being. The patterns of the Oriental carpets, the disorder of the hundreds of books spilling over from the bookshelves, these things, too, reflect the complexity of his personality.

"Acceptance comes so hard because everyone's private fears work against these theories, isn't that so?" I asked.

"Minna, that is true. I know that must be true, for why else would the entire scientific community react with so much anger, as if I had attacked their own families? Because they do feel attacked."

"Perhaps it is that their unconscious minds see the truth in your theories, so consciously they fight even harder to keep that knowledge below the surface," I commented.

"That would make sense, yes. When Josef Breuer was treating Anna O., he maintained to me all along that there was no sexual aspect to that case at all. Yet when Anna relapsed, her symptom was a hysterical pregnancy in which she fantasized that Josef was the father of her child! At first, that incident seemed to have convinced Josef, but later he denied it, refuting our book. I did not understand why he could not admit that Anna had fallen in love with him. It is such a common phenomenon among patients, particularly with female patients. We called it 'transference,' and even wondered whether this reaction facilitated the treatment. Anna's case clearly supported our work, yet Josef retreated from the truth. Why would his conscious mind need to fight it?" Sigmund paused sadly, lighting another cigar.

I hesitated for a moment, trying to make my thoughts more clear. Finally I said, surprising myself, "Do you think it is possible that Josef was in love with Anna?"

Sigi looked startled. "I had not thought of that, Minna, but now I remember that Josef was terribly slow in writing up Anna's case. It truly seemed as if he was resisting it. And during that same time Mathilde, his wife, seemed unusually unhappy. Several times when I stopped at their house, I found her crying, but she would never tell me what was wrong. Josef passed it off as nerves. Yes," he said thoughtfully, pulling at his beard, "that would fit. If he had reason to be frightened by his own emotional involvement . . ."

". . . his vision would have been clouded," I finished.

We sat quietly for a moment, listening to the wheels of a carriage clatter on the cobblestones in the street.

"And yet it still won't help," I said finally. "You and Josef are not speaking. Understanding why it is that your work troubles the world will not make the world less troubled, but perhaps one day it will."

Sigi's only answer was a deep sigh.

# June 2, 1896

This Sunday afternoon, Sigmund and I took the children to the Prater to watch the beginning of construction on the Wurstelprater, a large amusement park where they are building a sixty-four-meter-high Riesenrad (a Ferris wheel). They say it will be completed by next year, although I can't imagine such a creation. The children were very excited about the metal wheels and gears and asked hundreds of questions about how and why it would operate, which of course we couldn't even begin to answer.

The day was warm and sunny; summer had finally arrived in full bloom. A soft, caressing wind was blowing. I do love this time of year, when the trees and flowers become so full and brilliant. A group of wandering minstrels approached the bench where we sat to rest — but Sigmund sent them away, saying he could not tolerate such frivolity.

He has been very short-tempered since the lecture. Although we all are trying to be understanding, he can say very cruel things sometimes. Martha stayed home today with little Anna, who has come down with a cold. We left her in tears after Sigmund had told her she was not a proper mother to allow the baby to become ill. I tried to speak with him about this while we were watching the children play, but he would not listen.

"My relationship with my wife does not concern you, Minna," he said sternly. "We existed very well for years without your meddling."

I was shocked and deeply hurt. Perhaps I was, after all, merely tolerated in their household, just the spinster sister. No matter what has happened in the past with Sigmund, I must remember my place in the future.

Many times I have thought of that night of the wedding, when we kissed. The memory has kept me warm and comforted and has given me great reserves of energy to keep the household running while Sigmund is in his black moods. Now, however, I wonder just what it meant. Surely I must have read more emotion into it than was really there.

These thoughts are like a wound in my heart. Although I try to put them out of my mind, I seem to keep recalling them and touching them to see if they are still so painful. I am terribly discouraged, wondering if there is any meaning to my life.

# June 7, 1896

Sigi has ordered a strange new instrument for us, a telephone, with which people can talk together over great distances. It was invented in America and looks like a big wooden box filled with wires, with a black mouthpiece and listening piece attached. He purchased one for us and one for Amalie and Jakob, so that if Jakob's illness grows worse we will be able to help quickly.

"Soon we will have electric lights as well," Sigmund told us jovially, but then, his expression changing, he added, "to further light up my work for my colleagues."

"I don't know if I like their greenish tint," I said doubtfully. "The streetlights off Kartnerstrasse are greenish anyway, but you do get pleasure in these new conveniences, don't you?" I thought, but did not say, that buying these luxuries helped him to assure himself that his family is not yet poor, that his work has not led us to ruin.

Martha, too, is very pleased to have such a modern convenience in her home. She talks of having a luncheon for a few of her friends so that they can see the telephone. Of course, we all know that it will never happen; we are still outcasts in society. No invitation would be accepted, even by close friends.

Next week, the family will begin a much-needed vacation in Bad Aussee, where I visited Sigi and Martha in their rented house last summer. Amalie and Jakob will vacation, as always, at Bad Ischl, the emperor's retreat, just fifteen kilometers away. At least once each day for the past week, one of us, either Sigi, Marty, or I, has said, "It will be good to get away from the city." Then we laugh because the comment has become so frequent it is almost like a joke.

Marty is sure that the country air will remove the last traces of her illness. Sigi says he will work even better after a rest and after he has been able to meet again with Wilhelm. For myself, I too am tired of introspection. It will be good for me to walk in the country, to stop this endless daydreaming, writing, and searching of my heart.

I am still in love with Sigmund but nothing has changed. Since our conversation in the Prater, I am sure that he has no such feelings for me. When I think too much about it, I grow discouraged. I feel as if I am in a kind of limbo because I do not know what I want or what is possible. Yet I feel that my place is here. I enjoy the children, the companionship of the family, and I know I am helpful to Marty. Perhaps that is my purpose in life; perhaps that is enough.

## June 14, 1896

At long last we have arrived at our vacation haven. The little cottage Sigi rented is beautiful, nestled in a small forest. Martha and I marveled at its Bavarian design; the intricate gingerbread carvings in the eaves and along the front porch and the red carved shutters framing each window.

The walls are white throughout and the floors beautifully finished light-colored wood. The furniture is of a simple design, also made from this wood, whose name I do not know, and is accented with bright-colored pillows and throw rugs. Sheer white curtains grace each window and float softly on the mountain breezes. It is a lovely change from our home in Vienna. I knew in an instant that we would all be happy here.

Immediately upon our arrival, the children announced that they were "positively famished." I prepared a lunch of Wiener schnitzel and a large fresh salad. Martha set the table with white crockery dishes she had found in the sideboard and the children brought in a big bouquet of wildflowers. It made the meal very festive. Even Sigi seemed to be more relaxed.

Annerl has five teeth now. She is beginning to crawl about on the floor. I marvel at her progress – much more so than Martha.

## June 17, 1896

Every day now is warm and sunny. Mathilde and Martin have been taking long "nature walks," as we call them; the others aren't old enough, but they play in the sand at the lakeside for hours. I am constantly awed by the majestic mountains, green below where the grass grows and bare white stone above. Everywhere the countryside is spotted with red and blue and white and yellow wildflowers. Yesterday, the children brought a huge bunch of daisies to Martha, who had stayed in her room all afternoon because of a headache.

Today she was feeling better and joined us for breakfast. It was our last breakfast with Sigi for several weeks as he returns to Vienna to finish a paper for Professor Hermann Nothnagel.

When Marty saw that I was preparing pancakes, she even volunteered to make *topfenfulle*, a cottage cheese filling, one of her favorites. It is what she and Sigi had for their first breakfast together, she told me. It was quite a gay meal, Mathilde and Martin chattering on excitedly about the frog they found yesterday, Oliver asking fearfully whether frogs bite, and the baby prattling happily away to herself. Also this morning Martin first publicly announced his intention to become a poet, though he had confided it to me secretly before. He recited a poem to the family that he called "Wise Animals' Conversations," but the only two lines I can recall are:

*"Hare," said the roe. "Does your throat still hurt when you swallow?"*

Sophie and Ernst were seized by the bright idea that if they mushed up their pancakes with their hands, they would be able to build with the substance — like building sandcastles — and it took a great effort of dissuasion on the part of the adults to convince them that it wouldn't work.

Sigmund will be back within a fortnight. Marty and I assured him that his "amusing crew" will get on fine while he is gone.

## June 18, 1896

Today is my thirty-first birthday. So many years for such little accomplishment. When will I become something or someone useful?

## June 21, 1896

I have kept my resolve not to daydream too much. When I am alone, I feel an odd sense of fullness. The fresh air is doing me good and in the mornings I awake refreshed, cheerful, and happy to be alive, though there is one odd thing: I never remember my dreams now, although ever since my childhood I have always remembered them clearly. Perhaps when Sigmund returns I will ask him about this change.

For now, though, country pleasures and the family are all I care about. Jana, a local girl, will be coming to watch the children several days a week, but for the most part, I will still be responsible for their care. I brought several books with me, but I am not sure I will want to read now. Maybe I will give up thinking altogether and just let the sun warm me!

The other day, in one of the tourist stores in the square, I bought a little baby carrier, the kind that American Indian women wear to carry their papooses on their backs. I think this afternoon I will try strapping Anna into it so that she and I can explore together. Perhaps I will even be able to convince Marty to come along. The fresh air and sunshine would be good for her health.

Marty is more relaxed with Sigmund absent. Although she still keeps to her room most days, she is much more cheerful. I can see clearly here how much his moods affect her.

## June 29, 1896

Sigi returned after a fortnight and the whole house is alive; without him, I am only waiting, just making the time pass as pleasantly as I am able. Only his presence makes life real.

The children raced to the door to greet him the moment they heard the carriage draw up, bringing bits of moss and rocks to show him. Even little Anna smiled and gurgled, delighted with the sudden lively activity.

Only Marty waited quietly in the background. Before his arrival, she had changed into a more formal dress and had combed her hair. Sigmund went to her first and kissed her, then he came and kissed me, very quickly and lightly. Our eyes met, however, and once again I found myself breathless. The same attraction was present. A tingle began in my middle and I blushed. I had missed him so.

# June 30, 1896

After our cheerful dinner last night, Martha once again retired to her room, pleading a headache. She looked pale and drawn, and there were shadows under her eyes again. I don't understand why Sigi's presence should affect her so. So rarely do we all sit together and visit. I can't imagine being tied to someone who does not welcome my company, and my heart goes out to Sigi.

After the children were tucked into bed, he invited me to play a game of tarok, just as we often do at home. We chose the room he is using as a study here, although it is really more of a morning room. In this cheerful place, he does not seem to miss the clutter that surrounds him in his study at home. There is no desk here, so we had a large dining table moved in for his work. A single straight-back chair, a cushioned bench, and a large leather armchair are the only other furnishings. I had offered to select some pictures and carpets to add more color to the room but Sigi said that the emptiness might clear his mind.

Little Anna (Annerl, as Sigi calls her) had missed her papa while he was gone. Often she would crawl onto the cushioned bench and fall asleep there, as if awaiting his return. She liked the floral pattern of the upholstery and would try to pick the flowers off the fabric with her chubby little fingers.

The evening was still but for a slight wind that lifted the sheer curtains with occasional gusts. I am amazed at the freshness of the air compared to the staleness we are used to in Vienna. I have been dreading our eventual return home, although apparently not for the same reasons as Sigmund.

As he dealt the cards, I studied his face, noting the lines etched in his forehead. "Wilhelm always supplies you with solid ground," I said, musing about their forthcoming congress. "Will you be meeting him in Berlin?"

"No, this time Salzburg, in the Alps. It's a midway point for us, and the beauty of the old castle is inspiring. Maybe I'll find a new figurine to add to my collection. The cobbled streets surrounding the castle are full of wonderful little antique shops. Unfortunately, I'll have to defer this pleasure until August." Sigmund sighed and rubbed at his eyes. "Holding back desires," he said softly. "I wonder how life would be without such restraints."

"Holding back – that seems to be what we constantly do," I agreed, my pulse quickening. "Without that we wouldn't be civilized."

"But probably a great deal healthier," Sigmund laughed, patting my cheek. "Meanwhile, Vienna calls me again."

"Stay here as long as you can before returning to Vienna," I urged him. "Walking along the mountain paths is so refreshing, and we need to put some color back into your face." I tenderly placed my hand over his. "Perhaps inspiration is not what you need – it's endurance."

Sigi smiled in agreement but there was a shadow of pain in his eyes. I wondered what he was pondering.

We continued going through the motions of our card game for a little while before I realized that he was not concentrating. "There is something more that is bothering you," I suggested cautiously.

"You can't imagine what it was like to be back in Vienna," he said, his voice low and full of emotion. "That deadly ostracism is continuing. It's been months now, and still none of my old colleagues will even converse with me when we meet. Bad enough that they don't agree with me, but for them not even to be willing to listen is agony." Sigmund put his head down on the table, and as I looked at him in this attitude of abandonment, it was as if I too felt the terrible chill of their rejection. I reached across to him, my hands working slowly at the tense muscles of his neck. In the sad silence, the crickets chirped their unchanging song.

After a short time, Sigi raised his tired face to me. "After a few days in Vienna," he said softly, "I went to Nothnagel for advice under the pretense of showing him the draft of my work on children's paralysis. He greeted me personally at the door. As I had not been in his home for some time, I was surprised to see pictures of his wife and children still hanging in the waiting room. You remember that his wife died in childbirth? And his eldest son killed himself sometime last year. Nothnagel, brave man, has been both mother and father to his brood.

"He asked knowledgeably all about my latest work, and I was heartened when he commented that he found the manuscript intriguing. Then he asked if he could make a suggestion. I answered rather cautiously, afraid to jeopardize this friendly discussion. He assured me that I have an excellent reputation as a researcher and clinician and my neurological work is well known. He suggested that if I were to announce my intention to concentrate exclusively upon neurology he was sure I would gain a large, challenging, and remunerative practice.

"I told him that I was presently available for neurological consultations, and he said that he was aware of that but that my other work had created the controversy. I became defensive and told him that if he was speaking of my lecture before the Society of Psychiatry and Neurology that that had been a presentation I had been invited to give and so the response had naturally surprised me. I told him that, in fact, it had distressed me more than I could express.

"He said he understood this and that he was dismayed when he heard of this hostile reaction to an invited guest. His theory is that I am threatening Krafft-Ebing's greatest and best-known theories on sexuality. Nothnagel sees my work as presenting interesting hypotheses that can be tested scientifically, but he believes that Krafft-Ebing is afraid – afraid that my theories are correct and could discredit his own. He arranged the lecture, but Nothnagel said he spoke to the doctors beforehand to undermine my work. So Wilhelm was right all along. The whole thing was planned." Sigmund's voice broke and he was silent for a moment. The entire house was still except for the ticking of the grandfather clock in the hallway. My throat ached and I longed to reach out to comfort him.

"Minna, what can I do?" he asked, looking up at me. "What can I possibly do? Nothnagel finished by telling me again to give up psychiatry, forget my theories, pay polite homage to Krafft-Ebing and his *Psychopathia Sexualis*. I know he means well." His voice rose with anger. "Give it all up and then I'll prosper – that's the only way to play the university's game!" He pounded his fist on the table and the cards scattered and fell to the floor.

"Sigi," I said, "you can't give it up."

Once more we were quiet, alone in our thoughts.

"I cannot tell Martha," he said. "She does not understand the importance of my work. She would want me to do whatever would make her life easier."

"I don't believe that is true," I said strongly. "When Grandpa Isaac was under attack, he said – `Hold fast to the good. Keep with your truth. If they do not see, others will come with better vision. Forget the *gehazis* who seek only the *shekels.*' Sigmund, you must take energy from your anger and turn it into creativity!"

He did not answer with words but pulled me from my chair to sit close beside him. So we stayed, holding each other silently in a tight embrace for what seemed to be hours. Then we parted, he for his room, the one he shares, and I for mine, alone.

My love, if only I can give you peace in your heart. I will shield you from their fear. You need not acknowledge my love – only accept it.

## July 8, 1896

Walking beside a trickling mountain stream with Sigi by my side and Anna in her infant sling on my back, I imagined we were a family and Anna my own child. The warm sun was beating down upon the brightly colored clumps of summer flowers that sprang up around white rocks. I breathed deeply of the fresh, warm odors. The earth was basking and glowing and I wished the moment would last forever. Sigmund found one flower different from all the others – its deep red center surrounded by petals of a brilliant purple edged with white. He took out my hairpin to clip the flower there, and, with my neat bun undone, the hair tumbled immodestly down my back. Sigi and I have not talked again about his discovery of the conspiracy against him, but I can tell that it still weighs upon him. In a way, it must be a relief to him to know for certain. Now at least we can understand how his old friends have been turned against him. At the same time, though, he is deeply saddened by learning the truth about Krafft-Ebing, whom he had always respected so much. I am afraid he feels increasingly hopeless. He knows now that no glowing discovery, no sudden coup, will change his fortune – not in Vienna. No, it will be a slow process, fraught with political struggles, before the world accepts him. I must keep reminding him that these political struggles cannot tarnish the essential importance of his work. His work is more important than ever! Tomorrow, with dread, he returns to Vienna. He feels a grim responsibility to finish the paper on children's paralysis, and he will do it, but his overwhelming desire is to return to his own experimenting and discoveries, painful as that is for him now that he feels so alone. It is remarkable to me the way he works, harder than anyone, yet he has not lost the ability to be gentle and playful, as he was on our walk today.

"Minna," he told me, standing back to admire the flower he'd fastened in my hair, "you are now the embodiment of summertime in the mountains! And the most lovely summer I have ever seen." He kissed my hand and a thrill raced through me.

Yes, the closeness between Sigi and me is growing. It is not merely the closeness of friends—the emotion that we feel with even a casual touch is proof of that, but I have resolved to stop daydreaming and will resist these thoughts.

## July 9, 1896

Sigi and I have stayed up late talking in his study almost every night since he came back from Vienna. We are growing to know each other so deeply. We talk about everything – our childhoods, our parents, even his early years with Marty and mine with Ignaz.

I am no longer shy to talk to him about the physical love Ignaz and I shared, for Sigi does not accept the conventional view of sexuality as shameful; he knows that it is not only important but also beautiful. He even said that he admired me for having had the courage to act on the strength of my feelings, as many are afraid to do. "It is only the weaklings who submit to society's restraints upon sexual freedom," he told me.

I remember my fear and intimidation with Ignaz during our lovemaking and now I wonder what it would be like to be with a man as free as Sigi. My hidden desires grow with each of these dangerous talks. I wonder if he knows.

When we talked about our childhoods, he told me that although he loves Jakob very much, he has always been closer to Amalie, and I told him how devastated I had been at Papa's death and that I had not felt really right or whole again until I fell in love with Ignaz.

"Marty had always been the strong one in the family, and she seemed even more confident after Papa's death, but perhaps now sorrow is catching up with her. I worry about her, Sigi."

"Yes," he answered thoughtfully, "Marty is seriously depressed, it's true. It is not an uncommon phenomenon, for a depression to occur after the birth of a child. I think we are doing all that can be done for her, you and I. You are being so helpful and relieving her of so many of her burdens. I think all she needs is to continue to rest and to be confident of our devotion."

Sigmund gazed at me and his face softened into kindness.

"Minna, Marty never saw herself as you see her. She never felt that she was strong. She saw only that there was a family who needed her, and she was forced to grow up quickly."

I was surprised. "Do you mean that she resented taking on Mama's role? It always seemed to me that she was so eager for it."

"I wouldn't say she resented it. She is too warmhearted for that, and you are right that in many ways she welcomed the opportunity to take care of you and your mama. The crisis brought out her strong maternal quality, but everyone needs to be taken care of sometime." Sigmund reached out his hand and tenderly brushed a stray hair back from my face. Softly, he continued, "This is her time."

I looked out the window into the light from a bright, full moon outlining the trees and brush in the forest. It seemed an unearthly beauty, with the limbs of pine trees swaying softly in the wind. My eyes filled with tears of love. I can never take Martha's place — I just could not hurt her so. "You are very good to her, Sigi. You are very understanding."

"She is my wife," Sigi answered simply, rising from his chair. "Once I was very much in love with her and I still love her dearly, though we have become more like old friends who give each other comfort. She has withdrawn from me in many ways now. The sexual side of her nature was never strong, and many social factors successfully stifled it, but you are different, Minna."

I blushed uncomfortably when he said that. As often before, I had to remind myself that for Sigi, talking about sex is as natural as talking about sadness or hunger. I wanted to ask if he thought that he and Marty were not well matched, but I could not. What he had said helped me to understand what I had seen between him and Marty. She often acts so much older than her age — after all, she is a year younger than Rosa, who has just become a newlywed. With Sigi and me it is different. Our intensely emotional natures and physical longings are so much alike. It seems wicked to say this now, and so unfaithful to the memory of my darling

Ignaz, but the thought has crossed my mind of how happy Sigi and I might have been if we had met first before he met Marty.

## July 23, 1896

Marty looked lovely this morning, wrapped in her rose silk dressing gown, her dark hair hanging in a braid down her back. Little curly wisps of short hair framed her face, and for the first time in many weeks she looked relaxed and rested. She was preparing breakfast for the children when I came into the kitchen. "Well, good morning!" I greeted her. "This is a nice surprise." Of late, Marty has been staying in bed most of the day except on the days when she goes to visit Jakob, and I have become accustomed to bringing meals to her.

She gave me a timid, faraway smile. "Anna has been fed already, too. Maybe I would feel stronger if I spent some time out-of-doors. The country air certainly seems to have made you blossom, Minna. Perhaps when Jana arrives, you and I could take a walk together."

"That would be wonderful," I agreed, happy to see her showing some interest in life. "I promised Martin and Malthilde that today I would go see a new cave they've discovered, but that can wait. Why don't you dress while I finish up here."

"You are such a good companion to the children, Minna," Marty said quietly as she left the room. She seemed fragile. I began to carry the dishes from the breakfast table to the sink, hoping that Marty was beginning to rise from her melancholy.

A few minutes later, Jana rapped on the door and Sophie ran to let her in. Jana is a good-hearted country girl, young and strong. This morning, she carried a basket heaped with berries from her garden.

"Tante Minna," Sophie called gleefully, "Jana has a surprise — berries!"

"They look beautiful! Why don't you help her wash them," I suggested, "while your mother and I go for a walk."

Marty returned, dressed in a simple white blouse and red skirt, and said hesitantly, "I'd like to take the baby in that sling that you bought, you know, to carry her in — if you wouldn't mind." She slipped on her shawl, though it was warm and sunny outside, and I took the sling from its hook near the door. Baby Anna smiled broadly and gurgled when she saw me. She likes going for walks.

Outside, at the top of the little grassy path that goes from our doorway down the hill toward town, I showed Marty how to wear the infant sling. When I began to fit Anna into it, to my surprise she began to cry. Marty quickly slipped out of the shoulder straps.

"What is it, baby? What's wrong?"

Anna kept crying, reaching out her arms to me.

"What's wrong? Doesn't baby want to ride with Mama?" Marty crooned.

"Maaaa Maaa," said Anna, between wails, still reaching her dimpled hands toward me. It was the first time she'd said a real word!

"No, Anna. No, baby. *This* is Mama. *I'm* Mama." Marty pointed at herself.

"Ma-ma. Ma-ma," Anna insisted, trying to twist around toward me. Finally, there was no way to quiet her except for me to carry her in the sling. It was an awkward moment for us both. I felt the color rising in my face.

We walked down the path and, at last, Marty broke the tense silence. "Minna, I've — I've wanted to thank you for all your help the past few months, especially here at Aussee."

"Oh, Marty, don't thank me. I know what a strain the family can be and it's a pleasure for me to help and be useful, especially after your illness."

"Well, yes. For a long time, it has been hard, but as you can see," wryly she indicated Anna, riding happily on my back, "I haven't been that much of a mother lately. I truly appreciate what you have done, Minna."

"Marty, I'm happy to be able to help."

"And yet, and yet it's so *hard* to see you taking charge, Minna." Martha's voice shook a little. She gazed off into the distance, unable to meet my eyes. "I'm so used to being the big sister, always taking care of you. I don't have the strength right now to be a good mother, but when I see you doing it so well, I feel jealous. I feel like I'm not needed anymore."

"Oh, Marty, that's not true! The children love you so much, I could never take your place. When Sophie ran to let Jana in this morning, the first thing she told her was 'Guess what! Guess what! Mama got up and cooked breakfast for us today!' and Erni and Ollie were beaming."

"Dear Minna, that's kind of you to say. I know the children love me, but lately – oh, I cannot explain myself. Something inside me seems to be closing off. I feel so unhappy and empty most of the time and I can't even hide it, even though I think I should. And you seem so happy lately. You are simply glowing – you seem so fulfilled, so at peace. When you first arrived last November, you were pale and shy, as if you were in mourning. Now you have changed. I can't help my envy."

"You're right, Marty, I am much happier now than I was when I was living with Mama. You know Mama's household – so dark and elegant, formal and respectable, those damask tablecloths and fine china every night. There is no laughter there, no life.

"Playing with the children and helping Sigmund with his work makes me feel young again. I am alive, Martha. I can be strong and useful. You gave me this opportunity."

"I'm glad the move has been so good for you, Minna. I really am, and certainly I don't know what I'd have done if you hadn't been here." Marty stopped suddenly to look at a flower. It was a purple flower, the kind Sigmund had pinned into my hair on our walk. "Look, Minna. This is Sigi's favorite flower, a *kohlerose*. They grow only in the wild, and always by themselves, never in bunches with others. He used to bring them to me whenever he could find them." She mused quietly for a minute, stroking the silky petals with her finger. "It is rather like Sigmund, a single flower being different from all the others, don't you think? Let's leave it here and hope Sigi finds this flower."

Feeling suddenly guilty, I shivered in the warm sunlight. This precious flower was a symbol of Sigi's devotion that used to belong to Martha.

"I only wanted to thank you, Minna," my sister continued. "I don't want to burden you with my melancholy because there really isn't any reason for it. I should be a very happy woman, and I'm sure I will be again soon." Her flat voice belied her cheerful words.

We hugged each other, then turned to make our way back around the mountain. We hadn't walked far at all – no farther than I usually walk with three-year-old Sophie. A bee buzzed past us and Martha started nervously.

"May I try carrying Anna again?" she asked shyly.

I slipped the infant carrier off my back, this time without even taking the baby out, positioned the straps comfortably on her slender shoulders, and then tied the longer straps around her waist. She laughed. "What a clever contraption!"

"Indian women have to work, even when their babies are very small, so they had to devise a way to care for them at the same time."

"Heavens! What stamina! And they go right on after their births, without even a rest, don't they?" Marty was impressed.

Anna, who had been snoozing peacefully as she rode on my back, woke up suddenly and again began to cry. She flailed her tiny feet against Marty's back and squirmed around frantically. "Maaa-maaa? Maaaaaa-maaaa?" When she saw me she quieted down for a moment, holding out her arms hopefully. "Maa-maa?" Sad little tears ran down her chubby round face.

Marty kept walking down the path, grim-faced. "She'll stop crying in a minute if we just ignore her."

I couldn't bear to hear the baby crying, but I knew Marty was right. I admit that part of me was thrilled that Anna's first word, "Mama," had been directed to me! Often I had allowed myself to daydream that Anna was mine—my own child, created with a man I loved, who loved me.

"Marty," I said, hoping to ease the tension, "do you know that she's never said a real word before? This is the first time she's ever said 'Mama'!"

"That's very good, but she's going to have to learn to say it to the right person," Marty said stiffly, not slowing her pace. Anna was still wailing, sobbing, and gasping for air; her mother walks with a rhythm slightly different from mine, and it was my walk that Anna was accustomed to and found soothing.

Finally, when I could bear the baby's crying no longer, I said with some anger, "Marty, please! One of us has got to stop and comfort her for a minute. This is silly. It is not fair to her and it's spoiling our walk."

Silently, she turned around so that I could lift off the carrier. When that was done, Anna quickly grew quiet. I picked her up and held her to my breast for a moment, and she gave a sigh of relief, the kind only a baby can manage, and said happily, "Ma-ma." I wiped her face with a corner of my skirt and she snuggled up around my neck, holding on tightly to the fabric of my dress.

Marty was hurrying ahead down the path now, much faster than she had been walking before.

I called to her and stumbled along with Anna in my arms, trying to catch up. "Marty? Please stop. I can't walk this fast with the baby."

She stopped abruptly and whirled about. Anger was flashing from her eyes and her color was high. "Aren't you satisfied yet? You've already got Sigi! You can't have my baby too!"

Her outburst took my breath away. Then, just as suddenly, she seemed to crumple. One moment she was standing there confronting me and the next she was sitting down on the warm grass with her shaking knees drawn up to her chest, her head down on her knees, and her long red skirt spread around her. "Forgive me, Minna. I don't know what I was thinking. Forgive me. I need your help." Her voice was muffled and quavering.

I was also shaking as I went to comfort her. My thoughts were confused, more pictures than thoughts. There was Sigi in his dark study, with the smell of cigars so strong; there was the precious purple flower he had given me; there he was laughing with delight at my jokes, listening to my ideas; and there was the scene of our single kiss after Rosa's wedding. I felt sick. Was I – am I – trying to take Marty's husband and baby from her? Am I robbing my sister of her family?

No! Is it my fault that she has no interest in Sigi's theories? I can never hear enough of his thoughts and ideas. They energize me and fill me with desire for life. He needs to share his work with someone. Is it my fault that she chooses to stay in bed all day, leaving the children to my care?

If Anna's birth had not been so difficult there never would have been any question of my taking over the baby's care, but Marty was so sick, so weak for days after the birth, and compassion, not malice, made me intervene. That filled me at the same time with conflicting feelings of guilt and self-righteousness. I searched harder for a tenderness in my voice and in my love.

I sat Anna on the grass, knelt down beside Marty, and put my arms around her.

"Minna?" Marty looked up at me, her cheeks wet and blotched

with crying. "Minna, I didn't mean what I said."

"I know you didn't mean it. Everything's all right," I crooned to her as I might have crooned to comfort a naughty child. We embraced, and as I held her my heart softened and I felt her suffering, her melancholy, saw her beauty and strength as tears filled my eyes. We sat on the grass, rocking back and forth until her sobbing turned to hiccups and her breathing finally slowed. Then, arm in arm and with Anna on my hip, we walked up the path to the door.

There Martha turned and kissed Anna's tear-streaked little face and was rewarded with a smile. She said exhaustedly, "Minna, if you don't mind, I'm going to my room to lie down."

"Of course, dear. You rest now," I told her. I patted Anna back to sleep and lovingly laid her in her crib. "Poor baby," I whispered defiantly. "Mama loves you."

"Tante Minna, Tante Minna! Can we go to the cave now, can we, please!" It was Martin and Mathilde, skipping up to me as I turned away from the crib.

For a moment I felt as tired as Marty, and I understood, but I didn't want to disappoint the children.

## July 25, 1896

Martha has been cool and distant since her outburst on the mountain. I know she is embarrassed by the feelings she revealed — however, we both know she spoke the truth. I am torn between the loyalty I feel to my sister and my love for Sigmund and little Anna.

I cannot — will not — speak to her about her accusations of my usurping her place with Anna. If she wants to be closer to her baby, she must pull herself together and make it happen. The child needs loving and mothering, and I will not deny her even if her natural mother does. I surprise myself with the protective feelings I have for this little one. It is truly as if she were my baby.

When Sigmund returns, I'm sure the situation will improve. Until then, we will go day by day. I hope he is not suffering too much in Vienna. I do miss him so and am eagerly awaiting his return.

## July 26, 1896

This afternoon, I took a long walk by myself into town. It is Martha's thirty-sixth birthday, and I wanted to find a gift for her. I had been looking forward to this brief respite of solitude. Caring for Martha and the children has become wearing during Sigmund's absence. I also hoped that Martha and I could regain a little closeness on this special day. I feel her resentment whenever I am caring for the baby.

The day was warm, and I was glad to finally reach the town. I had worn my most comfortable walking shoes but even so found relief in sitting down to tea. Refreshed by the tea and pastry, I began to wander through some of the little shops. In addition to Martha's birthday gift, I did so want to bring back some little gifts for everyone. The young clerk at the shop where I had purchased Anna's infant carrier remembered me and we had a carefree time together looking through her stock for just the right things. For Martha she suggested a lovely crocheted lace collar, ivory in color, that will go beautifully with her new maroon dress. It will soften her features becomingly, I think. It seems to me that she dresses too severely these days. For the girls, I purchased brightly colored hair ribbons — even a lavender one for baby Anna, whose hair is beginning to grow in soft ringlets. I bought each of the boys a small hard rubber ball that could bounce very high. For myself, I found a beautiful tortoiseshell comb. It was an extravagance, costing ten gulden, but I do not allow myself many frivolities.

I am awaiting Sigmund's return with great anticipation and have begun to count the days. I have already chosen a dress to complement my new hair comb in preparation for dinner on the night of his return.

Before the children were put to bed this evening, they presented their mother with a bouquet of wildflowers that they had gathered while I was in town, and each gently kissed her on the cheek. She was touched by their simple show of affection and was much more loving toward them than she had been in days. She tucked them each safely into bed.

Martha accepted my gift of the lace but did not return my embrace. Sigmund sent no word to his wife on her birthday.

## August 1, 1896

"Now you children must behave because Grandpa Jakob isn't feeling well," I admonished. "Sophie, don't hit Ollie! Ollie, give Ernst back his necktie. Next year, you will be big enough to wear one, too. Martin, have you remembered the poem?"

"Yes, Tante Minna. I have it right here. Do you want to hear it again?" He started, "Hare . . ."

"No, I'll hear it again when you read it to Grandpa Jakob and Grandma Amalie." I settled back in the carriage seat, feeling relieved that Jana was taking care of Anna for the day. Mathilde had been invited to go hiking and picnicking with friends. A rented carriage filled with two women and four children is difficult enough! We were loaded down with presents of a drawing from Mathilde, a bouquet of forget-me-nots that Marty was clutching tightly, and a huge basket of food Jana had prepared: *Tevfelszungen*, devil's-tongue cookies, a cold goulash, a big pot of potato salad, and a special *striezel* — braided bread loaf — from a recipe handed down in Jana's family.

The hour's ride from Bad Aussee to Bad Ischl was very pleasant. Of course, the children were just beginning to settle in and stop squirming when we reached the outskirts of town. Jakob and Amalie have rented a lovely little cottage this year, set beside a small pond noisy with squabbling ducks and geese and graced by one apologetic-looking dignified black swan.

"Come in, come in!" Amalie was waiting eagerly at the gate for our arrival. She kissed us each soundly. "Martha, how good to see you again so soon. Jakob will be so pleased. Go right in, he's in the sitting room, dear. Martin, I would swear that you look bigger now than — when was it, two weeks ago? Sophie, what a lovely hair ribbon, my dear! And Ernst! Your tie! Ollie, don't look so woebegone, I haven't forgotten you, darling. I've saved a special hug just for you. Minna, you look lovely. Your color is wonderful. I believe the mountain air has done you a world of good. It does the same for me, I find. When I can pull Jakob away from his books, he always says nothing makes him feel better than a good brisk walk through the countryside. Children, hurry in! There's a big bowl full of *Schlosserbuben* waiting! You must be hungry from your trip." She went on chattering as we followed her inside. "And do you know, they have opened a new bakeshop here, just last week, and they make the best torte, better even than in Vienna! "Martha, dear, do you remember Frau Linweiss down the street, her youngest daughter was pregnant? Well, last Thursday she had a baby boy, weighed eight pounds and six ounces, and the whole family is so relieved, for you know, Minna, there is a history of anemia and babies born underweight in their family. Our other neighbor, Frau Feitgluchen, says she . . ."

Now we were all inside the cool, dark house and Jakob, who seemed to have grown still thinner, rose unsteadily to greet us. Sophie ran up to hug him first, hurling herself against his legs. "Grandpa Jakob! Grandpa Jakob! Will you read me a storybook later, the one about the princess?"

"Mathilde, my eyes are a little tired. Let me spend some time just looking at all of you."

"This is Sophie, Grandpa," Martin corrected. "Mathilde is not here."

Jakob looked uncomfortable. "Ah, my mind is starting to play tricks on me lately. It seems all my memories run together. I am sorry, children. I guess old age is catching up with me." Ollie uneasily grasped at my hand, hiding behind my skirt.

"Well, even if your memory is not what it used to be, you still have more wisdom in your little finger than most people have in their whole head," Martha said vehemently.

"Look at the wonderful treats we have brought and the children each has a present for you," I quickly said as Marty thrust her wilting flowers into Jakob's blue-veined hand. Trembling a little, he almost dropped them but finally managed to take hold of the damp stems.

"Thank you, darling Martha," he said hoarsely. "With my memory the way it is, for a moment I had some difficulty remembering the name of these lovely forget-me-nots." He shook his head ruefully.

We all laughed and the tension dissolved. Marty sat down beside Jakob on the couch and held his trembling hand as they began to talk. I followed Amalie into the kitchen to unpack our basket, which was almost bursting with food.

"Martin, Ernst, Sophie, and Ollie, you can all go out to the pond and play with the ducks for a while," I told them. "Martin, will you make sure the little ones don't fall in?" He nodded seriously and then they all ran out through the kitchen door in an excited rush, letting it slam shut as the last child left. I could hear Sophie wailing, "Wait for me! You're going too fast!"

"How is Jakob's health?" I asked Amalie when we finally were alone in the kitchen.

"Sometimes I have great hope," she said softly. "There are days when he seems to be the old Jakob I married — witty, amusing, and with all those wonderful memories of the past. Sometimes he even has the energy for a walk."

She unwrapped the *striezel* and sniffed it appreciatively. "The butter is in a pail in the back of the ice chest. Could you get it for me, dear?" Then she sighed. "But other times he doesn't know where he is or even what day it is. He gets lost in the past. Do you remember when Crown Prince Rudolf killed himself, along with that girl — whatever her name was?"

"Mary Vetsera, I believe, back in 1889 at their hunting lodge, wasn't it?"

"Yes. Jakob remembers that very clearly, but he thinks it was last year instead of seven years ago. Of course, his loss of memory is the least of it. Worse is when he awakens at three in the morning wheezing and gasping for breath. He has a lot of trouble sleeping, too, and sometimes during the day he cannot chew right, the coordination stops, and he starts to choke. It's so very frightening. I have to be careful to prepare food that goes down easily and isn't hard to chew."

She began to pour water into heavy drinking glasses. "He said he was feeling a bit better today. He was looking forward to this visit so much, you know. It means a lot to him, being able to see his family. I think the baths here may be doing him some good. Now, wherever did you get this *striezel*, my dear? With lemon rind, is it?"

"Yes, lemon rind and raisins. It's an old family recipe from Jana, the girl who has been helping us in Aussee."

"Oh yes, Marty has mentioned her, and she is good with the baby, too? Splendid. Yes, I think the baths and mountain air here do Jakob more good than any doctor, except Sigmund, of course. You know, Vienna was never Jakob's choice of a place to live."

"Yes. Sigmund said you moved to Vienna for his schooling."

"That is right. I was so concerned that he get the best education." She stopped to wipe her hands on a towel and looked up at me questioningly. "Sigi must have told you quite a bit about his childhood, then. I suppose you and he have gotten quite close."

"Well, I am very interested in his work," I said shyly. "We often play tarok together." I was relieved to have come up with this inoffensive fact.

"Oh, the tarok! Wonderful! It can't tell you as much as the tarot, but it is a game that is like life, with its chances and risks."

"Yes, that's what Sigi says, too," I agreed, laughing, "and each card is so beautiful."

Amalie hunted through a low cabinet for a bread plate. She said in a muffled voice, "Jakob has been concerned about Martha. She does not look at all well these days. It is very important, you know, that she takes a lot of rest. You should try to keep troubling matters away from her, dear, all you can."

"Oh yes, I know. I do the best I can to shield her from Sigmund's tempers and the children's energy. It cannot be a completely quiet household, as you know, but is there something in particular that worries you, Amalie?"

"No," she said thoughtfully in still a lower voice. "Only that illness in the family may increase the strain on Martha. If Jakob – well, I think Martha takes Jakob's illness very hard. They have always been very close. Of course, Sigmund and the children really need you, too. I believe you are far more important to Sigi than you know."

I tried not to blush and could not meet her gaze as together we covered the table with an embroidered white linen tablecloth.

"Your sister made this for me before she was married," Amalie told me proudly. "See how the color has held for all of these years."

Marty came in to join us and said laughingly, "In the days when I was waiting to see Sigi again, I didn't have much to do besides embroider pretty things." I was pleased she had come in just then, when Amalie was praising her. Together, we quickly set the dishes and tasty food in place and I called the children in from outside.

Jakob sat down ceremoniously at the head of the long walnut table, with Amalie at the other end, Marty to Jakob's right, and I to the right of Amalie. The eager faces of the children all around us seemed to light up the room.

Softly, Jakob asked, "When will Sigmund be returning?" and Martha answered.

"He will be back in a fortnight. He has a meeting with Dr. Wilhelm Fliess, you remember, his Berlin friend. It seems as if Sigmund never stops working, even when we are vacationing. Perhaps if he received a university appointment, he could slow down."

"I do not worry about Sigmund," Jakob replied, his voice a little slurred. "He is the oldest of this family, and he will carry on. The family is his strength. The children are his blessings, as is his wife, and as are you, Minna." As he uttered these last words, a sudden attack of choking seized Jakob and he began to gasp for air. The children looked as frightened as we all felt.

Amalie leapt from her chair, which overturned with a crash as she ran to her husband's side. Leaning over him, she slapped his back. "Breathe, Jakob! Breathe!" she urged him, putting all the force of her love into her voice. It seemed as if we all had stopped breathing too.

Finally the worst was over, and Jakob looked around, smiling apologetically.

"Well, thank God there's no need for a doctor this time," Amalie said. She was as white as a bed sheet. "He's had these attacks before, haven't you, dear?" She closed Jakob's trembling fingers around a water glass and helped him take a sip.

Suddenly he began to cough again, and I became alarmed when he seemed to be turning blue, but gradually the paroxysm lessened until he was only wheezing a little.

The children were frozen in place. "Grandpa, please don't die!" implored Sophie, bursting into tears.

"Hush, Sophie!" said Amalie quickly, and I said more sharply than I intended, "He's not dying, Sophie! It's only a coughing spell."

"Grandpa is much better now," Amalie said quietly, still studying his face. Then she patted his shoulder affectionately and returned to right her chair and sit down. That seemed to reassure the children, although it was plain that the crisis had exhausted her. Martin cautiously began to tell us about the ducks at the pond and then the other children started chattering, bidding for their grandmother's attention.

Martha had been silent throughout Jakob's attack, and now I noticed her pallor. She sat very still, as if she did not dare to move.

Jakob also saw her anxiety, for he said, "Whatever happens, Martha, you must remember to turn to God for your strength, and know that, with your wonderful family, you will have help."

I was relieved when the meal finally ended, and Jakob blessed the bread with the familiar old Hebrew prayer. He had to stop often to get his breath, clearing his throat noisily, but no one interrupted. When he was finished, we all left the table silently.

Martha confessed to me later as we washed the dinner dishes that, like the children, she had been afraid Jakob would die. Instead of feeling any emotion, though, her fear had so frozen her that she had become unable to feel anything at all.

"I was empty of everything, Minna. Suddenly I felt blank, as if I were made of stone. It was horrifying. If he should die ..." Her voice trailed off as she began to softly weep.

## August 3, 1896

It is late and I am sitting in a comfortable chair near the open door of my room. The breeze outside is cool tonight and the moonlight once again is glorious. Sigmund has not yet returned. Every day is an eternity without his presence.

I cannot stop mulling over the talk I had with Amalie later in the day of our visit to Sigi's parents. For reasons that should be plain, it was a talk that I think I will never forget, not as long as I live and am blessed with sound memory.

While Jakob was napping and Martha was with the children beside the pond, Amalie and I sat down together in the kitchen over tea. I sensed that she needed to talk, and I was not sorry for the chance to get to know Sigmund's mother better. She began to speak of Jakob and of their lives together, trying not to dwell on the sad fact that soon he would leave her a widow.

"Since my seven children have grown and left home, I have been enjoying city life in Vienna more and more, Minna," she said. "I read the cards in the Café Herzog each afternoon and listen to the band play waltzes at the Kursalon in the Stadt Park. If only I had a partner, I could join the dancers!" Bravely, she tried to laugh. "You should join me there some afternoon. We would have a wonderful time together."

Then she began to tell me about her colorful childhood. Her father, Joseph, had settled in Vienna to sell textiles and clothing after wandering through Poland and southeast Russia. He was descended from Talmudic scholars and cherished in his heart a great love of books, much as my family had done. If circumstances had granted him years and freedom, Joseph might have become a great writer such as Nathan Halevy Charmatz, a relative of his whose works Amalie remembers her father quoting, but he turned to textiles to make his living, and then he died young, when he was only thirty-nine and Amalie thirteen.

"Mama thought Vienna too dangerous because of the revolution," she told me. "Her brother had a small business in Freiburg, Moravia, a so-called free mountain town, so we moved the following year.

"It was a prosperous place then, and, although it was mostly Catholic, with a tall Gothic steeple at the town center, it was friendly to Jews. I loved the mountains and hiked whenever I could while Mama was busy with the younger children. I regretted that my education had to stop, but Father had been my teacher and I learned a lot from him. Wild mushrooms and truffles grew in the field behind our house and I used to spend hours there with my basket to gather them, imagining that I was a gypsy who would use them for magic spells or potions. Mama taught me how to clean and cook them, preparing me to be a good wife, as she had been."

"You must have had many suitors, Amalie," I said, thinking of how beautiful she must have been in her younger days.

"Yes, well, boys my own age never interested me; they seemed so silly and juvenile. When I met Jakob Freud, he was more than forty and I not yet twenty, but I was intrigued. He had had two sons by his first wife. There was Emmanuel, who was three years older than I, and Phillip, who was close to my own age. Jakob's first wife died in 1852, and his second wife, Rebekah, went in childbirth the year before we met. Although he was still grieving, he seemed gentle and kind, an older man with tenderness and experience, so different from the boys that used to court me.

"I had many possibilities for marriage, you know," Amalie went on with a proud little toss of her head. "I knew that I had an attractive figure and clothing and that I was something of a clever talker and a charmer, and then, when I turned twenty, I chose Jakob, and almost immediately after we married I became pregnant with Sigmund. While Jakob worked I had time to think and dream, to read the Bible and the Kabbalah. In the Kabbalah dreams are what the soul sees when it travels free of the body, but upon the soul's return the dream is seen through the body, and each person sees a dream in his own way. My father taught me that."

It seemed a good time to ask her about Sigi's birth, seeing that this was a moment that might not come again to learn about him what only his mother could know. Also, I could see that our talk was relaxing her, and I was glad. She seemed older today from the great strain of Jakob's illness.

"Sigmund," she said proudly, "was born in a caul, with the membranes still intact over his head. 'A great man has been born,' the gypsy Sofia told me then. When I saw his dark hair, I called him my little Blackamoor, but the name Sigismund came from Jakob's father, who had died just two months before his birth.

"I was so delighted with my son! It was an afternoon birth, and by nine o'clock that evening, I felt strong enough to begin caring for him. His nanny, Hannah Kutkus, a good Catholic woman, nursed him devotedly for his first two years, and we even let her take him to church — until we found out that she had been stealing from us." Amalie sighed. "Perhaps I was too harsh, ordering her out and telling the police. Dear Sigi missed her terribly at first."

"You only did what you thought was best, I'm sure," I said reassuringly.

"Well, I suppose that is so. In any event, by the time Anna was born I knew that we would have to move. Finances in Freiburg had become difficult. Jakob's business was affected by the railroad situation, and even the town schools were closing. Jakob suggested we move to Leipzig, where his brother had settled, and, after casting the tarot to see if conditions were favorable, I agreed. But in the end, we only stayed there for three months because work was scarce there, too, and I didn't like the weather.

"I believe it was in June that I cast the cards again, and this time the indications were sure. The card of travel and the card showing song, just after I had read about the Vienna Opera!" Her lovely weathered face warmed with a reminiscent smile, but then it grew sad again as she excused herself to see if Jakob was all right.

I walked to the window deep in thought and saw Martha and the children playing by the pond. This is how life should be – mother with children, devoted wife with husband. My relationship with Sigmund could never be like this – never so right.

The sun went behind a cloud, and I searched the horizon, fearful of rain on our trip back to Bad Aussee. A storm clearly was brewing, and distant thunder could be heard rumbling in the air.

When Amalie returned to the kitchen, satisfied that Jakob was still sleeping soundly, she refilled our cups of tea, took a deep breath, and seemed eager to resume her story.

"I am sure Sigi still remembers our move to the Jewish quarter of Vienna, Leopoldstadt. I never liked those cramped, plain apartment houses with their small, stuffy rooms. Four families had to share the bathroom and there was no hot water, but there were compensations for the discomfort. The best was that Jakob was able to earn enough money for us to be comfortable. Poverty is so hard on children and I wanted Sigmund to have the best of everything."

"Sigmund must have had a strong will as a child," I said teasingly, thinking of his strong character now.

"Oh yes!" Amalie said, laughing. "He had an opinion on everything, and what a talker!

"When we moved from Glockengasse to a six-room apartment on Taborstrasse, life became easier. We were nearer to Sigi's school, and he was doing so well – first in his class for six of his eight years at the Leopoldstadt Communal Real-Gymnasium. He showed so much promise that we gave him a separate room for his study. That made Anna jealous and she cried and cried later when we sold the piano, but Sigi needed quiet to concentrate on his schoolwork.

"You know, I always wanted him to study medicine. It is such a respected and secure profession. But his later interest in neurology did surprise me. Of course, I was very proud of him, but it always seemed to me that he could have set up a very nice family practice and then he wouldn't have had any financial problems. He wanted to write and do research, though, so that is what he did. What matters most to me is that he is happy.

"And now I am so pleased that you have come to help Martha, Minna." She looked at me sincerely and with great kindness as she said this. "She can give him much of what I gave him when he was young, a quiet place to work and a well-kept home. It's true that he needs those things, but he needs so much more. In many ways, you know, you are better suited to offer him those other things, with your education and love of learning. I hope you are happy." She finished rather nervously, perhaps feeling that she was being disloyal to Martha.

As for me, I could not help but feel that somehow she was saying that she knows of my feelings and even in some way approves. Sigmund's well-being has always come first with her — at whatever cost to anyone, including herself. If only I could turn back time. We would have made such a perfect match, Sigmund and I — even Amalie thinks so, and then Anna too would be mine.

I am tired and I must not let myself think such things. Tomorrow, in the sunlight, such shameful thoughts will be gone, but how my body aches with missing him.

## August 14, 1896

I hesitate to record my thoughts — even here in my most private diary. The events of today must never be exposed to anyone, least of all to Martha.

It is very late, and I sit here in my room listening to the silence. My mind keeps running in circles, and I truly believe I will burst if I do not release this torrent of emotions that is crushing me.

Tomorrow we must return to Vienna. I dread returning to the dark rooms of the apartment, with their heavy draperies, and to the harsh noise and bustle of the city.

Earlier today, Sigi and I took our last walk of the summer. We followed a mountain stream as it wound down and around the green hills. Much of the time we were quiet. We had stayed up late for the past several nights as he told me all about his congress with Wilhelm. Now it was enough just to be walking together in the sunshine. Words seemed unnecessary.

After some miles, the path began a sharp downward slant, and soon we were in a lush valley surrounded by hills and trees and brilliant flowers. It was idyllic, so beautiful. I said, without thinking, "I am so happy."

"Yes," Sigi said, "and I am, too. I feel a peace and inner harmony, Minna, that I have not felt in years."

After he said this, I was silent and shy and found myself walking ahead of him, as if to escape. This was dangerous talk, I knew, even if it made me so happy to guess – to know – the meaning behind his words.

We had reached a place where the stream poured itself into a large pond with water lilies floating on a surface of clear turquoise water. Sigmund came up behind me and, as we watched, several little fish broke the surface of the water, jumping and swimming as if in play.

"See there," he said, playful himself, "the fish are as happy as we are. They are such little fish. What are they? Minnows? Like you are, Minna. My Minnow."

Everything stopped and I could not speak. How could he have known? Of course, he hadn't known. It was only a pet name. Sigmund was only playing. Yet the name took me back so many years.

"Minnow" is what Papa always called me.

The next instant, I felt a rush of love for Sigi so strong and powerful I could barely control myself. Never have I so wanted to throw myself into his arms, touch him and feel him kiss me and caress me and say my name. I felt paralyzed for an instant by the strength of my desire and then by my fear of my desire. I heard myself talking nonsense.

"Sigi, let's stay here forever. Let's never go back."

He laughed, a low, soft sound. "Minna, you have the heart of a child, and I adore it. Let's stay here for the afternoon and make believe we are never going back."

My feet suddenly sank deeper into the soft grass at the muddy edge of the pond. I lost my balance and fell into his arms.

He caught me and held me so tightly that for a moment I could not breathe. Warmth coursed through me and the world fell away. Time stood still. I looked into his eyes and knew that we could not remain apart any longer.

My body and soul sing with love and passion for Sigmund. He was everything I had imagined a man could be. Of course, this can never happen again. We had agreed so on our walk back. But I tremble with the memory of our love in the warm sunshine. I will never forget.

## 19 Bergasse, Vienna

## August 15, 1896

We arrived home late this afternoon. I am exhausted from traveling. The children were all tired, but still it was very difficult to get them to sleep. They complained that their beds felt strange and that it was far too noisy with the city sounds to ever be able to fall asleep. Martha was fairly quivering with thoughts of all that must be done to get the household running properly again. I must retire early and be well rested for I sense that the next few days will be very difficult.

We received the sad news that Rosa had suffered a miscarriage while we were away. Sigmund is worried about her health. I shall have to visit her within the next few days.

## August 30, 1896

Sophie is sick with influenza and Martin has just begun to recover from another throat infection. Anna has not been sleeping well for several nights. I believe she may be cutting some more teeth, with her grand total at present numbering only six. I must remember to ask Martha what she used for the older children when they were teething. Anna falls asleep easily when I rock her in my arms, but when she is returned to her cradle, she cries. Last night, we cuddled together in the rocking chair and both fell asleep, not waking up until morning. Martha says I will spoil her. None of the other children were held while they slept, but Anna is different. She is mine.

The older children are to return to school tomorrow. Martin is apprehensive at the prospect. We have heard dismal but not unexpected news that they will begin separating the Jewish children from the others in each classroom. Sigmund has instructed Martin not to show any emotion at this offense. He said that his children must accept what it means to be a Jew.

I have tried to foster in the children a pride in their Jewish heritage, and, with Martha's approval, we've begun to observe some of the orthodox rituals I grew up with. I know that Sigmund hates it, as he does

74

not like any religion at all, but he has not yet stopped us. I am surprised at how much I have missed these little observances and customs. Perhaps Martha and I, together, will be able to influence Sigmund — never, of course, to keep a kosher home but to allow the smaller things, such as serving challah bread at the Shabbat table.

## September 17, 1896

This is Martha and Sigmund's ninth wedding anniversary. I had imagined that they would have a special evening—perhaps attend the opera or visit the theatre—but the only show of recognition of the date was a toast of wine at the dinner table.

Sigmund cleared his throat and stood beside the table. "To my lovely wife and our beautiful children," he said, smiling at everyone seated. That was all.

I asked Martha about it as we were clearing the table. "Don't you want to celebrate your anniversary?"

"Oh, Minna, you are such a romantic," she said, somewhat defensively. "Sigmund and I have been together for nine years. That is celebration enough. You will find, when you marry some day, that after children arrive things must change. The excitement and bloom of romance are gone, and a comfortable, stable relationship takes its place." At that moment, she sounded just like Mama. We finished washing the dishes without much conversation.

It worries me — this lack of emotion in Martha. I cannot believe that after a mere nine years passion must die. Sigmund's passion is certainly still unquenched. I remember well. But what is wrong with her?

If it were my anniversary, mine with Sigmund, we would be dancing the night away. The stars and the moon would shine with our love, and when we returned home late at night, we would celebrate in a very private way.

I am afraid my life is destined to be lived as I would like to live it only between the covers of this diary. At least here I can laugh and love with Sigmund without any fear of being discovered. In my real life, I must remember that I do not belong to him, that the children are not mine, and that this home is not mine. I should not allow myself to be filled with such despair – but my tears bring me rudely back to reality. My bed is empty – as am I.

## October 8, 1896

Martha and I received a note from Mama this morning. She has severely sprained her wrist and asked if one of us could care for her until it heals. I had assumed that I would go, leaving Martha with the children and Sigmund, but she was quite annoyed by my assumption.

We were in the sitting room going through the day's mail and planning the week's dinner menu. The weather was cold and cloudy, not at all uplifting to the spirit. A draft from the corner window whistled ever so softly and added a chill to the room.

Martha jumped up abruptly from her chair and began to pace before the coal stove. "Don't you think I am strong enough to care for Mama?" she asked, with sarcasm in her voice. "I certainly managed well enough after Papa died, and it is obvious that I'm not needed here."

"For goodness sake, Martha, you know that is not so. I just assumed that you would want to stay with your family." I stood and reached out to touch her shoulder, trying to make peace, but she stepped aside to avoid me. "If you want to go, and Sigmund does not object, I will be happy to care for the children and keep the household running while you are gone." Martha bit her lip and slowly shook her head. "I am sorry, Minna dear. I don't know what makes me so upset." She walked to the window and pulled the lace curtain aside, a lonely figure against the gray sky. "I think I need to be away for a while. Away from the children and, well . . . ," she paused, "from everything."

Did she mean Sigmund? My pulse raced – she couldn't know about us. I have been so careful not to give any hint of my feelings for Sigi. I took a deep breath, ready to be confronted with the truth, but she did not speak for several moments. Hesitantly, I approached her and gently embraced her.

"I want to see Mama. Can you understand?" she whispered, turning around to face me, tears beginning to show in her dull eyes. Her chin quivered as she fought to hold them back.

"Yes," I said quickly. "Of course." I patted her back reassuringly.

"I will take care of everything while you are gone." Relief flooded through me. Of course she did not know. She must never know.

## October 11, 1896

Martha left this morning. She will be gone for nearly six weeks, caring for Mama and then visiting with the Fleiss family in Berlin. I have not dared to think too much about this long time Sigi and I will have alone together. When I do, my heart races and my palms grow damp.

Marty gathered the children around her last night, like a hen gathering her brood of chicks. They sat on the floor at her feet with sleepy faces, wondering what was happening.

"I must go away for a while, children," she began slowly, in a calm voice. "Grandmother Bernays has hurt her wrist and she needs someone to care for her. She has been alone for so long – she needs someone to talk to, too – but I won't stay away too long, and your Tante Minna will take good care of you while I am gone."

Mathilde fiddled nervously with the hem of her skirt and I wondered what was going through her childish mind.

Martha went on to tell them to be good for me and to care for their father in her absence. The children sat still, not speaking for a few moments, then Ernst blurted out, "Is Grandmother Bernays going to die? My friend Franz at school says that all old people die. His grandparents all died one right after another."

Martha looked touched and concerned, reaching out for Ernst's hand. "No, child, of course not. Your Grandmother Bernays is very healthy. It's only her wrist that hurts. Of course, all people must die sometime – it is a fact of life. You all know that Grandfather Jakob is very ill and his time may be near. But I have not seen Grandmother Bernays for several years now, and she is my own mama. So I will help her just until her wrist heals and then I'll come home."

Reassured that a catastrophe was not about to befall the family, the children relaxed and began to ask excited questions about Marty's trip: Would she take a train or ride in a carriage? How long would it take to get there? What presents would she bring back for them? Only Mathilde was silent.

She stayed until the others had left the room and said softly to her mother, "I'll miss you, Mama," while little tears rolled down her round face. "Please," she begged, "can't I go with you? I promise not to talk too much and I'll go to sleep whenever you tell me. I could help with Grandma when you are too tired or your head aches." The little girl's pleading was heartbreaking.

"Ah, Mathilde," Marty said, gathering the child into her lap. "I love you, dear child. I will return very soon. You must stay and help Tante Minna with Anna." They went on talking softly to one another, as only a mother and child can do, until finally Martha set Mathilde down with a little tickle and the girl skipped off, seemingly quite happy again.

It has been months since I have seen such softness in Marty. Perhaps just the prospect of leaving has begun to release her from the heaviness that has possessed her for so long.

## October 13, 1896

Sigmund insisted on hiring a domestic girl – Josephine is her name – to help with the children while Martha is gone. I know that he cannot afford to do so but he refused to listen to reason, saying my time is much better spent helping with the translations of his work. I confess it will be pleasant to have some of the children's care shared, but I am uncomfortable whenever I think of our financial straits.

## October 17, 1896

I have not allowed myself to write my true feelings here since Sigmund and Martha's anniversary one month ago. For days after, I wandered about in a shadow that only now has begun to lift through useful occupation with Sigi's work and time spent with the children. Once again, I can see the sunshine and hear the birds (what few there are in Vienna) singing, but I must remind myself not to escape into the world of impossible dreams, especially during Martha's absence.

I have been enjoying my explorations of Vienna more since our return. My senses seem to have been freed during our time in Bad Aussee, and now I see so many things that I had not noticed before.

The architecture here is breathtaking. Bergasse, "the mountain street," our street, lies outside the Ring and has rows of five-story apartment buildings with sculpted facades. These are beautiful in their own way but nothing like the grand architecture along Ringstrasse.

This afternoon I accompanied Sigi on his daily constitutional while Josephine cared for the children. The day was clear and the sun warmed us, although the air has begun to grow crisp and autumnlike. It was cool in the shadows of buildings and I was glad to have my light wool shawl wrapped about my shoulders. It was a gift from Mama on one of my last birthdays. Its swirling paisley pattern has the colors of fall, brown with golden hues, like the few brittle leaves left on the trees.

Instead of making his usual circle around the Ring, Sigi led me toward "the little Danube," the Donau Canal, and we passed the plaza and entered the Tandlemarket. The smell of roasting chestnuts and potatoes wafted through the air. Sigmund bought me a steamy *burenwurst* with *senf* to eat as we walked. The streets were filled with vendors, and on the corners organ-grinders played for pennies. Their music mingled with the calls of the used-clothing vendors and the sounds of the new electric trams as well as with the familiar clop-clopping of horses. I loved the feeling of movement and life and felt my spirits lifting.

Everywhere good things to eat tempted the sharpening appetites of passersby. The apple vendor followed us down the cobblestone streets, offering luscious "red ones," and all the cafés seemed to beckon, especially the Konditoreis, with high-piled platters of tantalizing creamy pastries that filled the front window. As we came to the Café Central on the Herrengasse, I suggested we go in for some refreshment and Sigi readily agreed.

The fragrant atmosphere emanating from pots of steaming coffee enveloped us as we stepped inside. Sigmund chose a table near the front window, and we sat at a respectable distance from each other across its marble top.

When he finally succeeded in getting the busy waiter's attention, he ordered a mélange for me and a *mokka* for himself. Only after being assured of its freshness did he suggest that I try a *gugelhupf*, a very tasty cake made with many eggs and with a hole in the middle. He teased me about not knowing what it was, as if I had made a lifelong habit of frequenting the coffeehouses. I think that sometimes he does not remember that I have been in Vienna for less than a year.

"Everywhere we go I see food, and it makes me hungry all the time!" I said after the waiter had left. I was feeling quite happy, almost giddy. "At home, we start out with a light breakfast, as you know, coffee or mélange, and some rolls and butter, and perhaps an egg. Then at ten o'clock the snacks begin: more bread and butter, more coffee, and some pastries. At midday, soup, meat, poultry, vegetables, potatoes, and always dessert, like those dumplings filled with fruit. Then usually the mid-afternoon snacks — more coffee, tea and sweets, and sometimes even sandwiches — cheese, caviar, smoked fish. Then comes our big evening meal, with the family together after the littlest children have been put to bed, with treats like that marinated asparagus last night or maybe artichokes and a good soup and main dish. If that were not enough, if one goes out to a café later in the evening, there is always more coffee and more rolls. It is just heavenly — except for the effect upon a woman's figure."

Sigmund laughed at this lively recital, catching my good humor. "You sound like a menu at the Alserhof," he teased. "I have not, however, noticed any unbecoming change in your figure." His eyes twinkled, but then growing more thoughtful, he added, "You are right, though. In Vienna food and drink provide some of the greatest pleasures we are permitted to have."

"Why should that be?" I asked as the waiter set down our coffee.

"You must remember that suckling was our earliest oral experience of pleasure. Perhaps food and drink help us to recapture that primal satisfaction."

"So you are suggesting that the sophisticated Viennese have never gotten beyond suckling?" I asked, laughing.

My *gugelhupf*, sprinkled with confectioner's sugar, had arrived on a heavy stoneware plate. The first bite was delicious, light and buttery. I said to Sigmund, teasingly, that I did not know how I had managed to live without this heavenly delicacy, but he was now gazing out the window, still musing about our more serious exchange.

"Do you see how we allow expression of the hunger instinct as intensely as we attempt suppression of the sexual instincts? There seems to be a balance," he continued in a softer voice.

"Why is that bad?"

"Bad? My dear Minna, it is neither good nor bad — it is just how it is. Oral pleasures are not bad in and of themselves. Much gratification can come by this means." His voice trailed off and he seemed to hesitate before some unspoken thought.

"Are you afraid of shocking me?" I asked boldly, surprising myself with this new gaiety and forwardness, but Sigmund seemed too lost in thought to notice.

"In any case," he went on, as though I had not spoken, "in sexuality we call the oral methods — oral-genital contact — a perversion, but only if it replaces the usual gratification. Anthropological evidence shows that all forms of sexuality have been practiced by human beings since recorded time began, and probably well before that, of course." Then his tone grew louder and caustic as he added, "Even if my colleagues in this stagnant town won't recognize that sex exists."

An older man seated at the table to our right looked up as if with shock at this statement, and I felt myself blush. Sigmund, as usual, did not appear to be aware of the curious gazes he sometimes provoked.

"Shall we continue our walk now?" I suggested. I reached across the table and gently touched his arm. Happy to be out in the cool, fresh air again, freed from the crowded atmosphere of the café, we strolled past Demels, on the Kohlmarket, its steamy windows showing yet more beautifully arrayed pastries and waitresses hurrying by in their long black dresses, white aprons, and white lacy bonnets. We were just able to see, seated at the small, round, tiled tables, many young women with their attentive suitors.

"Minna, please do not be angry with me," Sigi abruptly ventured in a timid tone most unlike him, "but I have thought more about your situation and I feel . . . . Well, you are such a desirable and loving young woman that marriage should not pass you by." He looked away, feigning interest in a roasted chestnut stand being wheeled alongside us.

I did not have to search for a reply. It came instantly to my lips. "Love will not pass me by, Sigi. Some day the time will be right." Readily as the words had come, I did not fully know what I meant, for as I said that, it sounded almost as if I were promising myself.

Sigmund turned and looked at me for just a moment. I saw a

whole range of unreadable emotions in his gentle brown eyes and the set of his lips. Was it love I saw? Or admiration? Or perhaps surprise at my silliness. He must think me a romantic fool.

His gaze had wandered past me, though, settling upon a frail little man in black who was having trouble making his way across the street.

"We must go," he said abruptly. "I am concerned about my father." Since we have returned from Bad Aussee, Jakob's condition has been more stable, though he is clearly still very ill. Sigmund had said just last Sunday, after his weekly visit, that his father would not last long.

Now we quickly traversed the Ringstrasse and hurried across Ferdinande Brucke, where the softer gas streetlights were beginning to be replaced with the harshness of electricity. Sigmund shuddered and pulled his coat more closely around him. "Looking at that old man I had a premonition. Jakob has lived to see so much, and what a wonderful man he is. I am afraid that too often I have taken him for granted."

He quickened his stride, oblivious to my smaller steps, and I almost had to run to keep up with him as he hurried along Taborstrasse. Then we were at the door of number 17, his parents' home. Amalie quickly answered our knock.

"The cards told me you were coming," she said with a wise and satisfied air. "I'm glad you finally arrived." She greeted us each with a kiss and held tightly to Sigmund for a moment. She appeared even more tired than when I had seen her last, and her shoulders stooped, as if bearing the weight of a terrible burden.

"How is Jakob?" Sigmund and I asked, almost as one.

"Weakening," she said briefly, and I could see the tears in her eyes. We followed her into the parlor, and Jakob, who had heard our voices, hobbled in, supporting himself with his cane. The whole house felt dismally hot and stuffy as only a sickroom can.

"My son, and Minna. What a pleasant surprise. Welcome," he rasped in a breathy voice.

"We stopped by to see you since our walk had taken us near here already," I quickly lied. "How are you feeling, Jakob?" Sigmund said nothing, preoccupied in evaluating his father's condition.

Jakob sank into a soft chair and leaned his cane against a nearby table. "If I said I felt like a young buck would you believe me?" His eyes still sparkled with life, although they were shadowed and appeared to have sunk into his face.

"My son, with God's help, I've lasted this long. I can't count on much more. I know the signs. My breath is getting shorter and shorter, and Dr. Pfeiffer says it's all part of the heart failure." Sigmund nodded thoughtfully but still remained silent.

"Can we get anything for you, Jakob?" I asked eagerly, to ease the tension and gloom.

"Only the family Bible, my dear." He motioned to the wall behind Sigi. "It's over there, on the bookshelf. See, the thick leather book that looks as if it has been through storms far worse than this one of mine." I brought it to him and he balanced the book on his bony knees. Opening the sacred book, Jakob ran his shaking index finger down the middle of the first page, where he pointed to some handwritten script. "Read this to me, Minna, dear, please."

I lifted the heavy book closer to the gaslight and read,"'My father Rabbi Schlomo of blessed memory, Son of Rabbi Ephraim Freud, entered into his heavenly home on the sixth day of this week, Friday, at four o'clock in the afternoon, and was buried in the town of Tis Minitz, where I was born. By Christian reckoning, he died on February 21 and was buried on February 23, 1856. Let him return to the dust and rest in peace in G-d's Kingdom.' " I paused. Sigmund had his arm around Amalie's shoulders, as if supporting her.

Jakob pointed to a paragraph further down this page, skipping over the accounts of his older sons' births. "Please go on," he urged me anxiously.

" ' My son Schlomo Sigismund was born on Tuesday, the first day of the month of Iar, at eleven o'clock in the morning, May 6, 1856. The Moel was Herr Samson Frankl, from Ostrau. The Godparents were Herr Lippa Horowitz and his sister Mirl, children of the Rabbi from Czernowitz. The Sandkat was Herr Samuel Samueli in Freiburg, Moravia. May Schlomo Sigismund have the glory of his grandfather.' " I finished reading, and we all looked at Jakob.

"When I die," he instructed, "I want you to write my death underneath the last entry, so it carries on – my father's death, Sigmund's birth, and my own death."

"Jakob," Amalie interrupted, "we don't need to discuss this now. Let the Lord take you in His own time, not according to your schedule."

Jakob laughed gently. "Amalie, you have always seen the sparkling lining of all clouds and refused to believe in their darker side, but take down these words anyway, Minna, for when I am called."

Reluctantly, Amalie brought a writing pad from a small desk in the hallway, and I wrote down his words.

"After I die, write this with a quill pen, in the Bible, which will then go to Sigi: 'Jakob Freud died on this day, after a full life with much love within it. Now, at the end of my life, I see even more clearly that Love is the greatest strength we have. Love is the action of God in man and woman. And Love has propelled me from place to place and has been the foundation of my wonderful family.

" 'While I have said little, I have seen much. Now my Sigmund will carry on as head of the family. His strength will grow, and if there is any life after death, if any spirits can return, as the Kabbalah has it, then let him look to me as a guiding light.

" 'My wife Amalie has shown me how good life can be, and I know I leave her amidst a loving family and with good friends. The Lord giveth and the Lord taketh away. Blessed be the name of the Lord.' "

My face was wet with tears as I finished copying down Jakob's words. What he said about love I believe with all my heart. Love is strength, love is God. Quietly, Sigi got up and he and Jakob embraced tightly for several long moments. Amalie, standing at the door, looked grief-stricken.

Sigmund and I walked home in the chilly dusk in silence. I could feel his pain. His face was pale and pinched-looking.

Now, late at night, a cold thought strikes me. Perhaps Jakob will die tonight.

## October 19, 1896

A pall has fallen over our household. Concern for Jakob is constant, a cloud weighing upon us all.

I tried to read the newspaper to divert my thoughts and learned that the new prince of Bulgaria, Ferdinand of Koburg, a former Austrian officer, has been recognized by Russia.

I try to keep current of such affairs, but of late, so fully occupied with the events of our lives, I know I have often failed to do so. I must keep up my outside interests – or I fear I might become as dull and uninformed as Marty.

She is still with Mama, whose wrist appears to be healing but very slowly. I hope this time away will help to lift the shadow from my sister's spirits.

## October 23, 1896

Jakob was right in believing that his end was near. Less than one week has passed since he dictated his epitaph. He died this evening after a high fever, stupor, and finally a hemorrhaging of the brain. Sigi and Amalie were at his side, each holding one of his hands, as he passed on.

I must sit shivah for the seven-day mourning period with the family. Martha, of course, was notified at once. It was decided that she would remain with Mama. I believe this decision is good, for I fear the emptiness in her soul will be intensified by Jakob's death.

I will miss the old man, as Sigmund always called him. His lightheartedness and his wisdom strengthened by his love of God meant more to all of us than he knew.

At Jakob's deathbed, before he lapsed into a coma, he motioned for me to bend down over him. Then he whispered in my ear his last words – a precious secret of wisdom that I can never share – not even here.

## October 24, 1896

Sigmund has always prided himself on having control of his emotions, but Jakob's death seems to have shattered that control.

"Such thoughts and feelings are welling up in me now, as if the floodgates of my mind have burst," he said late last night when I tried to comfort him. When, at last, I left him alone in his study, as he had requested, I could hear him pacing and weeping all night long. At breakfast, he appeared haggard, more weary than I have ever seen him. The lines of his face were deepened by sorrow and shadows were smudged under his eyes. My own grief is deep, but I know I must set it aside if I am to help the others as they need.

Today, a short letter arrived from Martha. It is as I had feared — she is frozen, suffering as she did that day at Bad Ischl, when Jakob had his coughing fit at the table. There is a lack of emotion in her writing that is disturbing, almost as disturbing as Sigmund's agony. I have the urge to shout at her, to shake her, to wake her up and make her feel.

Please, please! I beg whatever powers there are. I cannot bear to see my family so broken with grief. Heal their hearts and souls, and grant me wisdom and patience to care for all of them.

## October 26, 1896

I have never seen Sigi so melancholy. It frightens me and reminds me of my own anguish after Papa's death.

Sigi has been talking about the deaths of all the men he has admired. Ernst Brucke, his mentor in physiological research, with whom he published five scientific papers, died in 1892, and the mourning Sigi says he held back is assailing him now. At that time, he was terribly busy with financial problems, his family, and a medical practice, but he named the baby born that year Ernst, in Brucke's memory, and he wrote to me then that Brucke had meant more to him than anyone else in his life. Now he torments himself with guilt, afraid he did not let himself feel Brucke's death deeply enough.

"Have I been a man without feelings? A monster in the name of science? What have I become? How could I not have been tortured then as I am now?" he raged this morning. "They have all been my teachers, my fathers. Have I been somehow like the Oedipus of myth — some childish part of me wanting their death?" His breakfast sat before him, cold and untouched. His appetite has always been light, but these last days he has hardly eaten at all, and his face has become thin and bony.

Then, as if obsessed with death and guilt, he began to speak of Ignaz's death, blaming himself for not having helped my beloved's consumption in time and for not having kept him from leaping to his death. He is grieving now, too, for his friend Nathan Weiss, whose arrogant attitude masked a deep insecurity and self-hatred, and for Jean Martin Charcot, whose work Sigi translated and who died in 1893, the year after Professor Theodor Meynert, the former head of the psychiatry department in Vienna. All teachers, mentors. In his grief, Sigmund has begun speaking and thinking of his own death as imminent, perhaps even as deserved.

We sat together in the sitting room after the older children were bundled off to school. Baby Anna crawled along the carpet, pulling herself up at every chair and table. Occasionally, she would burble a baby noise and seemed quite pleased with herself, but her father sat slumped in a chair, unnoticing, unmoving except for a nervous twitch of his fingers. He watched Anna's progress with unseeing eyes.

"We never know the bonds that connect our fathers and ourselves," he murmured despairingly, "until our fathers are gone. With Jakob's death, I have an overpowering feeling that I should have died, too." Tears filled his dark eyes, and suddenly he reached out for Anna and clutched her tightly to his chest until she protested with a squeal.

"Sigi," I said with love and compassion in my voice, "you are only forty. Jakob was more than twice that age. He was ready to die. He had lived a full life. It was true what he had me write in the Bible."

"I know you are trying to reason with me, Minna, but my grief will hear no reason. I feel as if I have been torn up by the roots, by roots I never even realized were there while my father lived." He shook his head sadly.

"But Jakob did not want us to grieve for him. He was serene in his death." The worn, brown-leather Bible rested on a marble table next to Sigmund's chair. I gently placed his hand upon it and began to recite, "After a full life with much love . . . ," remembering word for word the last entry in the Bible. But Sigmund interrupted me impatiently. "Minna, I know that, but none of it can help. His serenity is not mine. I must try to look to him as a guiding light, just as he said, to try to reach his eternal spirit. Now I know how much I have to learn from him. Now I need him, more than ever before."

With that, he got up, stumbling with weariness, and abruptly left the room. Little Anarel gazed after him, surprised, and waved good-bye to the empty doorway.

## November 2, 1896

Sigi has become obsessed with his search for spiritual guidance. Late at night, the light shining through a crack under the door of his bedroom wakes me. He has begun to write down his dreams, and he keeps a store of paper and pens near his bedside for this purpose. He also insisted that a board be placed under his mattress, saying he dreamed more when the bed was firmer. Today, he told me that he is working on a new theory, a theory of dreams and what they mean. During his blackest period of grief, a rush of new ideas came to him.

"I believe there are messages in my dreams," he said, staring at me intently.

"From Jakob? From Jakob's spirit?" I asked somewhat uncomfortably, shifting in my chair.

"No, from deep within my own mind, from the part of my thinking that is not conscious. Dreams may come like distortions of reality, they may seem like nonsense, but I am convinced there is meaning – important meaning – in them."

"Perhaps I should start keeping records of my dreams, too, so you will have more dreams to study," I suggested, a little hesitantly. I had remembered some dreams of my own that had made a strong impression and that had stubbornly clung to me for a long time. I began to feel intrigued by Sigi's idea.

He smiled, the first smile, I think, since Jakob's passing. "Yes, that would be helpful. You must write them down as soon as you awaken, though, before you have time to forget any details. I believe the details may work like a code. Even something that seems totally irrelevant may prove to be the key."

The sorrow of Jakob's death still hovers over our quiet house, but we are grateful that Amalie has been receiving much comfort from her children and her friends. She looked tired but not so strained when Rosa and I visited with her yesterday.

Poor Sigi, almost with desperation, has thrown himself into his manuscript about children's paralysis. It is now several hundred pages long. He is such a perfectionist that, although he is thoroughly tired of the work, he will not turn it over to Nothnagel until he feels he has given it his best.

I urged him not to work so hard, to allow himself time to recover from his father's death, but perhaps I was wrong.

"The work blocks my grief, Minna," he replied quietly but with conviction, "and I must go on. The family must continue."

Patients in the morning, the manuscript in the afternoon, and his own work at night. Yet somehow he finds the energy for it all.

## November 7, 1896

I see that Sigmund has increased his use of cocaine lately by the many empty bottles in the wastebasket in his study. He will not discuss it, but his nasal stuffiness and the occasional needle marks on his arms make it plain. He has become almost driven in his desire to complete the manuscript. Night after night, he sits up until the small hours of the morning writing and rewriting page after page.

After the children are tucked in for the night, I come quietly into his study to read or do my needlepoint as he works. There together, often in silence, we share a warm closeness of companionship that nourishes the flame of my love.

With Martha still away the household is more relaxed, even in our grief. Although the boys ask about her almost daily, the children seem to be thriving. Their normal bickering and fighting seem to have lessened, leaving a wonderful air of cooperation and even — although they would never admit it — love between them.

My little Anna is talking more and more. She does not seem to miss Martha at all.

## November 9, 1896

It is early in the morning. The sky is showing the first pale rays of the sun. I have been unable to sleep for hours. I tell myself that I should feel great shame, and indeed, I do feel it, yet something within me is proud. I feel fulfilled. I am a woman, a real woman with a bursting heart and an eager body, and I have given both wholly to the man I love.

This evening when, in my concern, I could not stop myself from mentioning the cocaine again, Sigmund suggested that I try some. It was late and the children were asleep. The house was quiet, I was with the man I loved, and I admit that I felt reckless. He injected a small amount of cocaine under the skin of my forearm and then he injected himself with a larger amount. Immediately, I felt light-headed, and then a great yearning took hold of me.

As the cocaine took effect, I realized for the first time that Sigmund's love and desire for me match my own for him. I felt his need stronger and undisguised now in his grief. I wanted to go to him, but somehow I could not move. I sat there on the couch, very still, quivering, waiting, and at last he sat down next to me. Slowly, he put his arms around me. He gently caressed my neck and my shoulders, then moved his hands down my back, saying, "Minna, Minna." I felt as if I were in a dream. We moved closer together, our embrace strong with the desire to melt into each other, to become one. Warmth passed through my body and I shuddered with pleasure. We fell back together and I forgot who I was, where I was — everything.

Now, in the privacy of my room, my guilt assails me and I cannot sleep. Once again, I have shared this secret, precious joy with my sister's husband and, no matter the love between us, I know that it is wrong. Marty trusts me, and again I have betrayed her.

Hours have passed, but my body is still radiant with sensation, my heart pounding so hard it is difficult for me to think. I will bring disgrace and shame to us all. I am an evil woman. I do not know what I will do.

## Evening

In rereading my last entry, written early this morning, I could still feel the warmth of his body. My heart is full of pain and aching. My eyes are tired and dry from lack of sleep. My mind is a turmoil of emotions.

Sigmund avoided my company all day long. Early in the morning, when I rose to bundle the children off to school, he was already shut away in his study. Yet I knew he could not be at work, as he may have wished me to believe. I knew that behind that oak door, so firmly shut against me, was a man as disturbed as I by the emotions we had stirred in each other.

Somehow he so contrived it that we did not encounter each other even once all day. So great was my pain at this that at last I felt nothing at all. My care of the children, my preparation of the family meals were performed as if in my sleep. I longed to bang on the study door and scream . . . but the last shreds of my dignity saved me.

Then we were all at the dinner table. Sigmund was there, near me, at last. I studied his face for the smallest sign, something that would ease this crushing pain, but he would not look at me or even speak to me directly. All the while, the children prattled on about their school-work and Sophie grew tearful over her doll losing some of its hair. I normally would have reached out to comfort her, but suddenly I knew I could bear no more. I nearly knocked over my chair in my haste to be away from them all and to be alone.

Now, in my room, I am writing all of this as quickly as possible — trying to empty myself of this anger and pain. All I want is to love him — and to be loved.

My hand is cramping — but the pounding of my heart is growing less. I must attend to the children. Please give me the strength to survive this evening. I must not let him see how hurt I am. I must not.

## November 10, 1896

Once again, a new day arrives. After the last pages and pages of pain, I must tell the rest to my only friend, this diary of my heart.

Last evening, after putting the children to bed, I was distractedly mending a tear in Ernst's brown wool trousers when Sigmund knocked on the door to my sitting room. My head was aching and I was perilously close to tears again.

"Minna," he said hesitantly, "I believe we need to talk about what happened." His manner was stiff and formal and his eyes still could not meet mine. I put down the mending, and my heart began to pound. I dreaded what he might say – knowing that however happy we had been last night, what we had done was terribly wrong.

"As you wish, Sigmund," I managed to whisper, my voice shaking. The room suddenly felt much too warm and the gaslight too bright. Perspiration pricked my back and my breathing was shallow and rapid – as if I could not find enough air. Sigmund's voice came to my ears as if through some sort of tunnel, yet I remember every word he said.

"I have dreamed about you, Minna, almost since you first came to live here nearly a year ago. I felt warmth, sympathy, and understanding radiate from you, and, yes, I was drawn to that, desperate for it. Yes, I love you, and especially in this time of despair I need you." He sat down heavily beside me and took my hand. I could hardly believe I was feeling his touch again, and I tried hard to steady my trembling.

"There is no harm in dreaming, is there?" His voice was gentle, a little self-mocking. "I thought I could channel the strength of my desire into my work, that when Marty returned she would be rested and renewed and the temptation would not be so strong, but now, what we have done again – I do not know how to set it right." His voice was almost pleading, as if he asked me what to do, and now it was I who, tense and ashamed, could not bear to speak or look at him.

For Sigmund, though, it was as if, now that he had spoken at last, he could not stop, and his words tumbled over each other in a passionate rush. "Minna, my dear Minna, look at me. My mind is churning like that of a man possessed. Yes, this is possession. I was carried away when I embraced you with a force over which I seemed to have no control. You wanted me, I think, yet it is true that I seduced you. I am the man, the decision was in *my* hands. Oh, Minna, I acted out of love and need, but again I have betrayed my wife, and you too, my dear Minna. You deserve a man who can love you openly; a marriage, a home, and a husband of your own. What can I offer you? Nothing."

In one desperate, violent movement, he released my hand and strode to the door.

I ran to him, throwing aside the last shreds of dignity, and fell to my knees, hiding my face in shame. "Sigmund, please!" I begged. "Please don't leave me like this! Yes, it was wrong, but I love you." For the first time, I had said it. I loved him and now he would leave me.

What relief when, after a frozen moment, he began to stroke my hair. Then, placing his hand under my arm, he helped me to rise and led me to the sofa. We sat there silently for a while, embracing, letting our breathing slow and our thoughts begin to take shape. The coal in the ceramic stove clunked softly as it burned down. The only other sound in the room, in the world, it seemed, was the quiet sound of our now softer breath. I felt as though our Maker, Himself, was listening and had silenced even the angels.

Sigi's tortured conscience would not let him accept the gift of this moment of perfect peace. Drawing back from me with a groan, he began to speak again, raising his hand when I tried to stop him. "Aging, poor, driven by my work, unrecognized – perhaps I am as misguided as my colleagues think. You deserve more than this, my Minna, and more than a quick tumble in the grass in the countryside or a furtive late-night grappling. I have only burdened you, complicated your life and my own in this clandestine drama.

"Try to understand my guilt. Marty, my wife, your sister – our children came too soon for her. She should not have aged as she has. I remember the fresh, sweet, trusting girl she was in our courtship, the girl to whom I poured out my heart in letter after letter all the time we were apart. The love we shared and the strength she gave me were precious and indestructible, or so I thought then. And yet, here I am, betraying it.

"And my practice, my reputation. If Rieger in Würzburg found out that I had slept with my sister-in-law, he could discredit me entirely. Already some profess to think of me as perverted, some kind of sex fiend.

Last week in Vienna, Rieger called my theories 'an old wives' psychiatry' and said my work made him shudder. And Krafft-Ebing! Krafft-Ebing would like nothing better than to see me flung into utter darkness. If a suspicion about us ever got about, Minna, he would fan it into a scandal to finish me off, to complete what he began with his malicious lecture invitation. And my father. What would he think of me now?"

A feeling of energy, of strength, began to overtake me, coiling tightly in my midsection and then rising up my spine. I could bear to hear no more. My hand flew to Sigmund's lips to silence him. A voice spoke from within me, perhaps from my very soul. It spoke the emotions that I could not release – and yet it spoke the truth. "Sigmund, what we have done is not right, but fate has brought us together for a reason. My lover died. I am barren. Your wife has borne you six children and she is tired. I can help with your work – and I can ease Martha's heavy burdens. Who are we to question what is meant to be?" I dared to look at him now. He sat silently with his dark head bowed down but his manner was a bit less desperate and I felt that he was listening. Surprised at my brazenness, I continued, well aware that I was risking everything that the world values – security, my good name – but what gave my words force was that I knew that these things were not everything to me.

"Anna is my baby, Sigmund," I said clearly and quietly. "I love her, and she needs me. You are all the husband now that I shall ever need. You are interested in my thoughts and you have said that you love me. What more will I ever need in life?" I paused, drawing in a deep breath. Tears were spilling down my face but I did not stop to wipe them away.

I felt his quieter, listening presence, and it seemed to me that everything had been resolved between us at last, even though he did not speak. "No one need ever know about us, Sigmund." I found myself kneeling again on the carpet before him. This time, however, I was the stronger one, the dominant force. Somehow, I had to persuade him, to reassure him, that this was right.

He looked up slowly and cupped my face in his soft hands, as though searching for the truth. "It is enough for me, Sigi. You must believe me, and Martha will not be hurt, I will see to that. She will never suspect that I am doing more than helping with your work, and she will be relieved that you do not make physical demands of her."

"Minna, my dear," he said finally, studying my face, "do you realize what you are sacrificing?"

"I realize that I cannot exist otherwise," I said. It was the truth. From deep within my soul those words had risen, and they brought with them a strength and sureness I had not before experienced.

Then he pulled me close and again we were together in a frenzy of emotion and release, but the difference this time was that something had been settled and pledged between us, and we both knew it. No longer was I afraid of chasing after him—of being rejected or chastised as a child might be. We were partners, for better or for worse.

So this, I see now, is my reason for being. No longer do I have to search for the meaning of my life. I will be with my love, and with Anna, and we will live together in harmony with the world. No one will know of this very private matter, hidden deep within our hearts.

Resting in my bed while I write this, my weary head is nestled in a pillow and I am wrapped warmly in a soft, downy quilt and am at peace with the world. No matter what happens in the future, I will be able to live with my conscience. Within this cocoon of our little family and of Sigmund's love, I can give my own love freely. To the outside I will be as always. And only Sigi and I will know.

## November 12, 1896

There was a gas explosion late last night that rocked the entire building. Being jolted out of bed, I ran immediately to Anna's crib — only to find that Josephine had already arrived there and was comforting the frightened baby. Sigmund and I nearly collided in the hallway when he went to see if the boys, "his monkeys," were all right, and I rushed in to reassure the older girls.

Apparently, there was a gas leak in the apartment below, resulting in the explosion. The poor man, a watchmaker, escaped disaster by scrambling out through a back window. How frightening it must have been for him.

Immediately this morning, I called to have our apartment inspected. I would not like to live through another such disaster.

## November 13, 1896

More good news today! The watchmaker has decided to give up his apartment. This means that Sigmund may take it as his office.

The extra room will be wonderful for the children — and I'm sure it will be excellent for Sigmund's work and concentration. The separation of working quarters from the living quarters will make me more comfortable, too, when we are together.

Even Martha will be pleased.

## November 15, 1896

We have settled into a comfortable routine, my family and I, while Marty is on her travels. The children seem to miss her but have been satisfied with the few letters they have received. Little Annerl does not seem to notice her absence.

Martha says in her letter that Mama seems frail, older. My sister is still grieving for Jakob, but she has left for the Fliess family home in Berlin by now and I am sure this will be a much happier atmosphere for her. Although there is much to do with the children and the household while she is absent, I am enjoying the freedom of managing things in my own way. I have even hired a new washerwoman. Sigmund has been unhappy with the state of his shirts for several months now, but Martha had formed an attachment to the older washerwoman who had been with us for some time and would not consider replacing her. I have chosen a young woman, well recommended, and am confident that she will do well.

It is so pleasant to hear the children run and play when they return from school. Martha was always hushing them, but I believe they need this freedom of expression. I know I should not be too critical of Martha's methods of child-rearing. After all, she has had full responsibility of the children for many years, but I do think she is a bit harsh with them sometimes. Perhaps when she returns refreshed and rested she will be able to better enjoy their zest and vitality.

## November 20, 1896

Preparations for Sigmund's office are progressing. The damage done by the explosion has been repaired. There are new locks and we have taken possession of the key. That makes it feel real.

Tomorrow I will begin to move his things down from upstairs, with the help of some hired men. Sigmund says that he will be out paying visits then. I know that the thought of his prized possessions being touched by strangers makes him very uncomfortable. I do hope I can have the entire suite arranged before he comes to see it. The middle stages of moving can be terrifying.

## November 22, 1896

The children and I made a ceremony of presenting Sigi with his new study. I placed a blindfold over his eyes, and the boys held his arms, guiding him down the steps. At the door, I placed the key in his hand and helped him to open the lock.

When the door swung open, I removed the blindfold. The waiting area is sparsely furnished, with a small grouping of tables and chairs. The walls are covered with a dark floral paper that emphasizes the dark wood floors. I had spaced pictures carefully on the walls and placed on the small bookshelf a few volumes I thought might be of interest to the patients.

On the wall opposite the entrance there are the double doors leading into the consulting room and, through this, the study. Sigi opened the door with a hesitancy that made me smile. The children all hung behind him, waiting for his reaction.

The richly colored Oriental carpets, covering the wooden floor, give the consulting room an exotic air. On the worn brown-leather reclining couch, with its customary Persian carpet draped over the back, I had piled a number of pillows, just as Sigi likes it. Here again, prints, paintings, and plaques are hung on finely lined maroon wallpaper, which makes a rich background. At the foot of the couch, tucked into a corner, a ceramic coal stove was warmly glowing.

I had set Sigmund's velvet armchair and footstool in the other corner, directly behind the head of the couch. He prefers this placement so as not to interfere with his patients' free association.

Next to the entry door to the consulting room is a small, inconspicuous door covered with the same dark wallpaper. This allows people to leave through the consulting room in privacy, without encountering the next patient, who may be sitting in the waiting room.

I had placed only two bookshelves in the consulting room, and these were both filled to capacity with Sigi's collection of Egyptian artifacts.

On the other wall is another double door, this one painted white, that leads to Sigmund's study. It is lined from ceiling to floor with bookshelves, except for one wall that has a large window facing out onto the courtyard. As in the consulting room, the nearly full bookshelves display antique statuettes.

Sigmund's desk, on which I had neatly arranged his papers, is near the window, as Sigi likes it to be, and the dark wood gleams from polishing. Along the front of the desk was a row of his most prized artifacts. There is a comfortable armchair across from the desk where I can sit for our talks.

Sigmund looked at everything, beaming with pleasure, and thanked me profusely. "I couldn't have done better myself, Minna," he said warmly after a quick embrace. The children entered carefully, almost afraid to tread on the beautiful carpet. They gazed around in awe until Josephine quietly ushered them back upstairs.

I am very happy that Sigmund approved of my work. He and I will spend many pleasant hours here.

## December 5, 1896

Sigi is exploring again old fields of interest — witchcraft and the occult. I have always found this area interesting, although I don't know very much about them. I've brought some of his books to my room to read late at night so that I can learn more.

He seems to work much more productively when we can discuss his projects together. It pleases me to be able to help him in this way. He frequently asks my opinion now, and I am flattered to see some of them reflected in his writing.

Josephine is doing extremely well with the children, and this has freed a good deal of my time for Sigmund. I do not know what will happen when Martha returns. There are a few more patients, so finances are not as tight. Perhaps we will be able to keep Josephine.

## December 12, 1896

Martha returned this morning, looking refreshed and rested. She was obviously happy to be home with her family. She brought gossip and news of Mama with fond remembrances from the Fliess family. I think the time away was just what she needed to restore her health.

She is thrilled with Sigmund's new office, as I knew she would be. Martha is not interested in his work, and having these offices at a greater distance from her wifely domain pleases her.

Josephine was a bit cool toward the mistress of the house. Perhaps she feels her position threatened. The children have taken a genuine liking to her. She and Martha will have to work things out. I cannot intervene because Martha already resents my attachment to Anna.

I believe I am beginning a migraine headache. (Sigmund has been free from his headaches for several weeks now.) Perhaps mine is being caused by Martha's return?

## December 22, 1896

We are once again preparing for the season of Hanukkah. This year, Martha and I have agreed to light the menorah regardless of what Sigmund says. I do not think he will protest, however. He still feels broken of spirit. I did hope that moving to his new quarters would revitalize his energies, but I believe he is still suffering terribly from Jakob's death.

The weather has been cold and clear. All of Vienna is decorated for the Christmas celebration. I enjoy this time of year more than any other. It is a time of such joy and happiness, such warmth and comfort. A time for families. I wish I could give to Sigi some of the warmth I feel in my heart.

## December 25, 1896

It is very late but I feel compelled to share the experiences of the evening.

Sigmund and I were discussing one of his new books, *The Malleus Maleficarum*, a book of witches and spells. I must admit that the idea of calling up the dead frightens me. It feels so unnatural.

He has decided to try some of the spells tomorrow night and swore me to secrecy. I feel I must be with him — for who knows what the result will be. We will wait until very late, after the household is asleep.

Sigi gave me a pendant to wear under my clothing and kept one for himself until our experimentations are finished. Mine is a carved mandrake talisman hung from a piece of twine. He said I must swirl it three times, counterclockwise, toward the heart. It is supposed to represent the phallus. His is a stone rose, the symbol for the vagina. He said we must wear around our necks what our bodies lack. Sigi explained that they had been treated with saltwater and special oils and anointed with rosemary. The talisman is supposed to protect one from the evils that may be wakened.

I fear he has experienced some kind of breakdown. There is an excitement in his voice that makes me uneasy. I dread what will happen tomorrow night.

## December 27, 1896

The events of last night were so bizarre that I can barely bring myself to write of them. Sigmund filled his study with small blue glass jars of incense, a mixture of patchouli, bay leaves, pine needles, wormwood and cloves, and a little olive oil and honey. He said it is called a "cernunnos incense." It is supposed to call down the powers of the planets. The smell was odd – unlike anything I had smelled before. It was both sweet and spicy and filled the air with a moist, thick scent.

On the floor he made a circle with string, surrounding both of us. It was seven feet in diameter, ringed with two larger circles. This was called the magic circle, and he said it was exorcised, safe from all harmful energies.

"The circle is a mystical shape used again and again in witchcraft. Another is the pyramid – a triangle, like this one with the green eye." He picked up a piece of paper. "This triangle is used to call back the spirits of the dead."

"Sigmund," I said nervously, "are you sure we should be doing this? After all, you don't know what will happen." It was a black night outside and the wind was whistling through the window in an eerie manner.

"Minna, Minna. Don't be frightened." He gave me an excited smile and a squeeze of my hand. "I know it seems strange, but these spells are images that have been used over centuries, throughout cultures. They are really no stranger than the distorted symbols in our dreams. What I want is to find out how they work, whether they call forth some energy of the mind."

Slightly reassured, I allowed him to continue explaining the odd things surrounding us. There was a lilting, rhythmic quality to his voice that was new. He spoke seriously, but his face appeared more serene than I had seen it in months. Perhaps this was necessary for his healing process, and maybe, just maybe, these experiments would give him a greater power of understanding those persons around him.

We crouched on the floor for hours, reciting and memorizing spells. Nothing remarkable happened. Finally, when the dawn's first light was coloring the sky, Sigmund decided to stop. I could tell that he was frustrated.

"Perhaps these take practice or time to work," I said, trying to ease his frustration.

"Possibly," he said negatively, "but it is also possible that I am just a failure at this too. Wouldn't Krafft-Ebing enjoy seeing this scenario?" he asked, waving his hand about the room filled with candles and strange symbols. His face was lined and worn in the flickering candlelight.

He spent the balance of the day alone in his study. I would like to encourage him in his exploration of witchcraft. The energy I felt from him last night was like that of the old Sigmund—daring and uncontrollable. A short break might be just what he needs. Perhaps a short trip tomorrow.

## December 28, 1896

I spoke first to Martha, telling her that Sigmund had reached a block in his writing, and she agreed that a day trip would be just the thing.

It took me all morning to wear down his resistance. I told him that the point he had reached in his work was exactly the reason why he should leave it for a while. "Avoid the staleness that plagues you so often! Haven't you learned yet that a good idea will continue to grow and grow if you don't push yourself too much? You are working to harness the power and messages of your unconscious. Well, your unconscious mind will be much freed, much more active, if it is not battling with your conscious mind all day."

Grumbling, he admitted that I might have a point. I am amused by how he can never quite admit that I am right. His response is always tinged with the slightest doubt.

Finally, we headed for the train station. We were going to the woods across the Alte Danube, at the point just before it merges with the Large Danube. There was a small inn there where we could lunch and then spend the day hiking and exploring the caves and the view from the Kahldenberg Mountain.

Sigi spoke very little, and my worries about him returned. I know how heavily Jakob's death still weighs on him. His grief has not abated. I only hope the guilt over our love is not burdening him as well. It scared me to see him so quiet, standing so stoop-shouldered, sitting with his legs drawn up taut and his hands folded tightly together on the train, his eyes looking inward.

The day was unseasonably warm and the sun shone brightly from a clear, perfectly still blue sky. The place where we would take a ferry across the river was just a short walk away through the fields of tall, dry grass.

We began walking briskly, but after a few steps, Sigi slowed down. He seemed to be ambling through the fields, as if we had no destination, and I felt impatient.

"Sigi, let's hurry," I urged, taking hold of his arm.

He placed his other hand over mine and responded, "Why are you hurrying so? You convinced me to take a vacation — now I am trying to take a vacation. Look at the birds above us," and he pointed up at two white doves circling in the sky.

"They are beautiful, Sigi, but I am anxious to get to the other side. It's even nicer there."

"But you miss so much by hurrying. Look!" He had stopped again, admiring a thick tree with a golden-colored bark, some yellow berries, and a few leaves. I was surprised to see him take out a small pocketknife and swiftly cut off a bright thick stick, leaving the leaves and berries on. "I can use this as a walking stick," he told me, obviously pleased with himself. I shivered, as this was so unlike Sigi — so unlike the solemn, purposeful, scientific man I knew.

We reached the ferry, slipping a bit at the muddy shore, and found that we were the only passengers there. The boatman, a heavyset older man, advised us in a gruff voice against crossing, telling us that it would storm later.

"Why do you want to go?" he asked in bewilderment, removing a faded blue cap and scratching at his balding head. "You'll be the only visitors there, and with the storm coming . . ."

We thought him ridiculous, looking up at the sky, which remained a clear, unwavering blue. "We will go ahead," Sigmund declared, stepping gingerly into the boat. He layed down his walking stick and reached out his hand to help me in. The boatman reluctantly began across the river.

As we reached the other side, a ferocious black dog came running up to the dock, barking furiously.

"Belongs to the caretaker," the boatman explained briefly. "He don't hurt no one as long as you keep 'im fed," and he pulled out an oil-spotted paper package and threw the dog some scraps of a sandwich, which quieted him down. He squinted suspiciously at us. "I'll be back at four this afternoon – but I won't wait 'ause of the storm," he warned. "If you aren't here when I get back here, you'll just have to spend the night." We nodded and thanked him and as soon as we were standing safely on the dock, he rowed off quickly, his oars making soft lapping sounds in the water.

"He was certainly strange," I commented to Sigi.

"You keep an eye out for that storm," Sigmund teased. "Actually, he knows the area much better than we do, and you must remember that it isn't the tourist season."

We walked along a winding path, breathing in deeply the fresh country air. I turned back to look at the river from the distance and, startled, called Sigi's attention to a huge billowy gray cloud that had gathered on the horizon.

"Sigi, maybe we should just go back. I hadn't realized how deserted it would be here." The approaching storm we hadn't believed existed made me feel frightened without knowing why.

Sigmund simply gave me a look of disbelief and grabbing my hand pulled me along the path. Further along, we saw the little brown-and-white thatched inn. I was delighted – it looked just like I had remembered it from years ago, but I recalled it being lively and noisy, full of vacationers. Now it was silent, deserted. The trees were bare and the ground covered with dull brown winter grass.

"I do hope it's not closed," I said worriedly.

"Yes, we're open! We're open!" called out a small older woman cheerfully as we walked in. "You'll be our only customers for the day. People usually stay away when it storms, you know." Sigi and I exchanged uneasy glances. "But I like to see people brave enough to give it a try, personally." She winked at us. "Yes, we stay open all year round. Would you mind signing the guest book, please?" She motioned to a small book open on a wooden table by the door.

Sigmund signed for both of us, printing more carefully than his usual large scrawl: Dr. Sigm. Freud, Fräulein M. Bernays.

"Why, Dr. Freud, I knew your father! I knew Jakob Freud very well indeed. He used to come here all the time. Used to sit right over there, that table in the corner, and we'd talk for hours."

I looked at Sigmund in surprise. "I didn't know that Jakob and Amalie ever came out here."

"I didn't either," Sigmund said, looking confused. "I think you must be mistaken, Madame. My father passed away a short time ago, but so far as I know he never visited this island. You must have him confused with someone else."

"No, no. It was Jakob Freud. I can see the resemblance. And he used to talk about you all the time. His son who was a famous doctor in Vienna. That is you, is it not?"

Sigmund shook his head. "I suppose it could have been, but was my mother, Amalie, with him?"

"No, he came alone – but you must excuse me." She stopped suddenly, giving a little half-curtsy. "I am Frau Dreyer, the owner of this inn, and of course on a day like today when we are not busy, I am the waitress, too." She smiled broadly at us. "And you must be Herr Doctor's wife, Minna."

Sigmund squeezed my arm, so I remained silent. A chill was running up and down my spine.

"You must be famished, and here I am prattling away. Please, come sit here at the table Jakob used to like."

"No, no," I said loudly and quickly before we could move. "We just stopped by to visit the inn. Come, Sigmund. We must go now. It was very nice to meet you." I turned without looking at Sigmund, and he followed me outside.

"I'm sorry. I hope you did not want to stay for lunch."

"No, Minna," he said. "How could she have known my father and so much about me? I simply cannot understand how he could have been here."

We walked quickly away, and I kept looking nervously over my shoulder, feeling someone's eyes on us. The sky was darkening rapidly and a chill wind had started whipping around. Against the blackening sky, a tall tree assumed an evil pose. Sigmund took my hand and held it tightly until he found what he wanted. Halfway up the hillside, set into the rock, was the small mouth of a cave. The sky opened and rain began falling in sheets. We were drenched by the time we reached the small shelter.

"Now what?" I asked, shaking.

"At least we are out of the storm here," Sigmund said. "You wanted a vacation," he teased with a gleam in his eye. "There is wood here to build a fire. We will be warm soon." He set to work and quickly a small fire was crackling cheerfully.

Sigi stood behind me and placed his arms around me. "Take off your clothes, Minna," he whispered. "They need to dry," he added before covering my neck with kisses.

We curled together on the ground, letting our clothes dry in the warmth of the fire. Both of us still wore the talismans around our necks. Sigmund reached over to his pack and pulled out a book of witch spells. I said nothing but listened intently as he began to chant. I remember feeling the heat of the fire on my face, the coolness of the ground beneath me, and I heard his slowed, even voice incanting "Jakob, Jakob. Remember me? Come to me, Father Jakob" over and over again. Then he called in a loud voice, "By the mysteries of the deep, by the power of the East, by the holy rites of Hecate, I call thee by the ties of love, Spirit of Jakob, break thy eternal fast with me, so mote it be."

I do not remember more as I believe I fell into a trance with Sigmund's lilting chants repeated endlessly. At one time, I thought I heard Jakob talking to Sigmund, but it may have just been Sigmund's voice. The words "Forgive yourself. Remember to love" echoed through my mind as I awoke from visions of myths, dragons, and strange beasts. Sigmund was sobbing quietly beside the glowing base of embers, all that remained of the fire. Outside, the storm had passed and the blinding sunshine illuminated our love. We dressed silently.

Together, Sigi and I made the surprisingly short journey back to the river. Sigi's walking bough was helpful, keeping us on the path, which was slippery with rain. When we reached the river, the boatman was waiting.

"I told you it would storm," he said, "but you went ahead anyway. Maybe you learned something, eh?"

The river crossing was quick and gentle and soon we were on the train going home. Sigmund broke the long silence.

"The hysteria theory is ruined, Minna. Finished. Not every hysteric has had early sexual experience."

"I'm sorry, Sigmund," I told him, truthfully.

"But all is well, Minna," he said, patting my hand reassuringly. "I was looking for an easy answer, one simple answer to hysteria. The truth is deep and winding and complex. I feel better about it and even relieved."

After a few minutes, he spoke again, this time in a softer, thoughtful voice. "Minna, witchcraft has similarities to hysteria. What we know as real is a fragment."

"What happened in the cave, Sigmund?" I asked hesitantly. "I'm not sure, Minna," he said, his voice breaking slightly.

"You called for Jakob."

"Yes, I called for him with every chant I knew. Did he come? Did I converse with my deepest self? I remember that I am to trust and not to judge until I understand. Well," he said, breaking into a laugh, "I'm far from understanding."

"But you will go on," I said, wondering about the events of the past days.

"Yes. I'll go on. I don't understand enough about the witchcraft to pursue it intently, Minna, but the dreams, the associations of my analysis, the path to my truth — the hardest is to come, but now I feel strength enough to do it."

"And I have strength to do it with you," I heard myself say.

# 1897

## January 17, 1897

Oscar and his wife Melanie left this morning after visiting with us for several days. It has been years since Martha and I have seen our brother. We spent most of the time reminiscing and talking about Mama. She is such a strong, domineering figure and has affected all of us in our adult lives.

Sigmund has kept mostly to himself. I hope he has not been feeling neglected while I've been with my brother.

The new year has begun with a pleasant start. Our family seems to be in total harmony.

## February 21, 1897

I have had a constant string of migraine headaches for the past four weeks. Anna has been my only consolation, placing her cool little hands on my throbbing forehead and kissing my aching head.

I've not been able to be much help to Sigmund or to Martha, for that matter. Why is our family plagued with these headaches? Sigmund and I seem to be most prone to them. They are so dreadful and unpleasant — I simply want to hide under my bed covers. Even the slightest light seems to make the pain increase. Sometimes when my eyes are closed, I see shooting lights — something like a star falling in the dark sky. I must ask Sigmund if he has ever experienced anything similar to this.

Thank goodness for the soft, snugly body of little Anna.

# March 1, 1897

Sigmund joined me late this morning in my parlor. I had been daydreaming, curled up next to the window. It was a cold, blustery day and the sound of the wind shrieking against the trees outside had made me a little melancholy. I sat with my cheek pressed against the cold window.

"I am meeting Schnitzler at the Café Mérkur, on Floriangasse, for lunch. Would you care to join me?" he asked, drawing a chair up beside me.

"Is it only Schnitzler you are meeting?" I asked. Arthur Schnitzler, a doctor and playwright, has visited our house several times. I like him but have at times felt a little left out during his conversations with Sigi. They shift back and forth between the medical world and the world of theatre so quickly that I find it difficult to follow.

"No. In fact, that is why I thought you might like to accompany me. Do you remember hearing Arthur talk about 'Frau Lou'? Lou Andreas-Salome?"

"Frau Lou? Is she the one Arthur said had an affair with Nietzsche?" My interest began to stir, thinking about what I had heard of Frau Lou.

"Yes, that's she." Sigmund looked slightly embarrassed. "Apparently, she and Arthur are more than friends now, as well, but she also has many other lovers. From the gossip I have heard, her sex life is enough to produce a scandal, yet she continues to be accepted in intellectual circles because she is an important author in her own right.

"Well, I don't know. I've never met her. She isn't in Vienna that often, and Arthur has been insisting that I should meet her for some time now. It seems that she is very interested in psychoanalysis."

"She must be very beautiful to attract so many lovers," I ventured, feeling a bit insecure.

"Yes, I have heard that she is. Well, what do you think? Why don't you come along. It should prove to be a very interesting lunch. Besides, it will get you back in touch with what's happening in the theatre, and you may get to hear some of the latest jokes."

I reluctantly agreed and went to change into a proper gown. In truth, I did not want Sigmund going alone to meet this fascinating, beautiful woman who sounded as if she lacked morals. I scolded myself as I dressed for having such a wifely thought, but I could not help feeling threatened by the idea of someone like Frau Lou. Our relationship was precarious enough without the influence of another woman.

I remember reading about her in the society paper, which Marty calls the gossip column, the *Wiener Tagblatt*. They referred to her as "Lou-Kind" —"Baby Lou" — and were always linking her name with one man or another. I had not known if I should believe it.

"So Lou is Arthur's new lady friend," I said as Sigmund and I started toward the café, my woolen scarf whipping around my face in the chill wind. "And Arthur is still a playboy?"

"Yes, for the most part. He keeps a diary of all his women and the number of times they make love. But Lou is not exclusively Arthur's. She is actually in Vienna to visit with Frederick Pineles, who is trying to be a nerve specialist at the Vienna Neurological Clinic. Pineles is eight years younger than she and one of her most recent lovers."

"She likes doctors, then?" I asked naughtily.

Sigmund laughed. "Have no fear, Minna. I am more than occupied with the women already in my life." He took my arm as we crossed a busy street. "I believe she is only thirty-four, just a little older than you, but do not get the wrong idea about her, Minna. She is not just a harlot sleeping with all these men. She seems to inspire each one to be his most creative during the time they are together. Friedrich Nietzsche has said that she changed his life."

We walked the remaining distance in silence, fighting against the cold wind. Maybe I did have something in common with Frau Lou after all. I was sure this would prove to be an interesting lunch.

The warm, steamy air revived us. Arthur and Lou were sitting at a table in the corner, where we spotted them immediately.

She was, indeed, as beautiful as I had feared. "Sigi! Fräulein Bernays!" Arthur greeted us. Sigmund and Arthur shook hands warmly while I waited, just slightly behind Sigi. "May I present Lou Andreas-Salome."

"Call me Lou-Kind. The other name is too long," Lou interjected quickly with a warm smile.

"And I am Minna," I added, sitting down in the chair Sigmund had pulled out for me. I removed my gloves carefully, trying not to look at her too obviously. She was very fair, with light hair and creamy, pale skin. Her eyes were large and expressive, blue-green in color, and her mouth rather wide but very becoming. I felt very big and plain sitting beside her.

"We took the liberty of ordering for you. We chose the special. Since the weather is so cold we thought you might want to eat as soon as possible when you arrived," Arthur said. "Gulyas soup, lamb's breast in marjoram, and a chocolate custard. Will that suit you?"

Sigmund acknowledged that it would be fine. I knew that I had to swallow my shyness and make a good impression. It was important to appear witty and charming.

"And what do you do, Martha?" Lou-Kind turned toward me.

"Minna," I corrected her, embarrassed. "Martha is my sister, Sigmund's wife."

"Oh, I see," she said, raising one eyebrow.

Hastily I continued, "I help care for the children, of course, and I like to read . . ."

"Minna has been a great help to me with my research and translations. She is fluent in English, German, and French," Sigmund interjected for me quickly, and I threw him a grateful glance.

"And do you find that rewarding? Living so much as a helpmate?" Lou-Kind's voice was soft, but I felt as if she was talking more for the men than for me, though it was me she addressed.

My face grew red. "Well, I find it rewarding to help Sigmund, yes. I believe his work is very important."

She dismissed this with a nod and a simple, "I see." Then, turning to Sigmund, she oozed with charm. "It is true that I have heard a great deal about your work, Sigi. May I call you Sigi? It is such a darling nickname!" She laughed girlishly and I found myself disliking her. Without waiting for an answer from Sigmund, she continued, "I was so interested when I heard about your theories on the importance of sexuality and bisexuality."

Sigmund was thus launched onto one of his favorite topics – the tracing of the masculine and feminine parts of each person. I burned with jealousy at Lou's ease in talking about sexual matters, and on a first meeting with a well-known man! I also fumed that Sigmund did not seem to be aware of her cunning and coquetry. The food was served and I busied myself with eating, remaining quiet as the conversation shifted to Arthur's newest play, *Liebelei*, now being produced at the Volkstheatre.

Lou leaned forward to make her point, and for the first time, I noticed that she seemed distinctly masculine in her conversation once she had stopped her flirtatious airs.

"Sigmund, you believe repressed sexuality is at the root of hysteria, true? Then if society was more open about sex, so there was no shame or repression surrounding the topic, then there would be no hysteria?"

Sigmund seemed taken aback. "Frau Lou," he said, and I noted with satisfaction that he had used her more formal name, "we do not have any way of knowing what such a society would be like or what it would produce. There is a chance that if sexual repression were loosened, culture would simply find a new object of repression. Besides that, all civilizations that we know of have had some taboos on sexual expression. The incest taboo, for example, is close to universal."

"Well, what stops us from making such a society to experiment?" Lou countered.

"Such a society would have to be economically self-sufficient, for the dominant civilization would not tolerate such deviance for long. In fact, Professor Fredericks in the philosophy department at the university told me of a place in America, some small community in New York, where that had been tried."

"Oh yes! The Oneida community," Arthur said. "My friend in the United States wrote that the community disbanded, and they made quite a scandal of it. He sent me clippings about it from the newspapers."

"Yes. It was a community of men and women who practiced a sort of 'group marriage.' Everyone had relations with everyone else and the idea was that in that way, sex would become part of people's normal everyday experiences, like eating and sleeping, and would lose the mystery associated with it but would gain a group intimacy," Sigmund explained animatedly. I had never heard him talk about this community before, and I was surprised to see his excitement. I knew that he considered such things terribly immoral, but as a scientist he seemed fascinated.

"What about babies and pregnancy?" Lou asked sardonically. "Did the men designing that great society think of that?"

"They practiced sex without male completion," Sigmund said.

"Easier said than done," Arthur chuckled, and Lou snapped, "That's right, Arthur! I have a feeling that such a society could be used as just another way to tie women down. Instead of having just one man to worry about being impregnated by, women would have multitudes. What kind of freedom is that?" Her eyes were fiery and I realized with surprise that this was no longer a purely intellectual discussion. "Don't you agree, Mary?" she suddenly asked me.

Taken by surprise, I could find nothing to say. Sigmund again spoke, oblivious to her anger. "But that is not the point. For about thirty years, everything went well. They were a fairly harmonious community, and their farming went well, but eventually the people in the local community refused to tolerate them and stopped trading with the farm. Economic starvation eventually broke it up."

"A parable of our times," Arthur said lightly.

"Arthur, my dear. King of irony." Lou leaned over and kissed him on the cheek.

Arthur laughed. "Dear Lou, I've gotten your claws out. Let us treat this all with humor." He turned to me. "Sigmund has told me that you share his interest in jokes."

"Yes, I enjoy them a great deal, and Sigi and I analyze them to try to figure out what makes people laugh. We've even discussed compiling a book on the subject," I said shyly.

"Tell us one," Arthur spurred.

I hesitated for a moment, but Sigmund motioned for me to do so. Somehow I felt like an animal displaying the tricks I had been taught. "Well," I began timidly, "you've heard of the *schadchen*, the marriage broker, who was defending the girl he proposed.

" 'I don't care for the mother-in-law,' the young man said, 'she's a disagreeable, stupid person.'

" 'But after all,' countered the *schadchen*, ' you're not marrying the mother-in-law.'

" 'But the daughter isn't young anymore and she's no beauty.'

" 'No matter,' said the *schadchen* with fervor. 'If she's neither young nor beautiful, she'll be all the more faithful to you.'

" 'And she hasn't much money.'

" 'Who's talking money? Are you marrying money or a wife?' asked the *schadchen*.

" 'But she has a hunchback, too,' said the young man.

" 'So what do you want? Isn't she entitled to have a single fault?' "

My story met with a mild laugh from Sigi and Arthur but with only a polite smile from Frau Lou.

"It's all-important to be a wife," she said sarcastically.

Arthur ignored her comment. "And how do you analyze such a joke?"

"This joke gets its laugh through faulty logic," I explained, glad to have this chance to discuss what Sigi and I had analyzed. "It is the appearance of logic by the *schadchen's* twisting of logic."

"Another!" Arthur demanded gleefully.

"Well, the easiest joke is a play on words that masks something deeper, like social inequality. Consider the poor man, Hirsch Hyasmith by name, who announces to his friends that he sat next to Salomon Rothschild and was treated as an equal – famillionairly."

At this even Frau Lou laughed, but she seemed to resent having the group's attention diverted away from her. Sigmund was beaming with pride at my forwardness.

Our dessert was served, and she reverted back to her vulnerable little-girl self, pretending to worry about her figure and wondering aloud whether she should allow herself a sweet. Of course, both Arthur and Sigmund's eyes had been roaming admiringly over her figure for the entire meal, and both of them now encouraged her to treat herself to the *göttermehlspeise* while she preened.

After dessert, the talk turned briefly again to relations between men and women: marriage, monogamy, abortion.

"I told my Andreas when we married that I would need to go on having other lovers and that if I became pregnant I would have abortions without hesitation," Lou said, tossing her hair back proudly. "My life is more important to me than the life of any man whom I am with."

I stirred my coffee slowly, glancing at Sigmund for his reaction. I could not read in his expression whether he was sincerely interested or slightly shocked. He made no effort to speak; however, he was hanging on every word she offered. Lou speaks in such a manner calculated to get

*116*

attention, yet she seems to have more conflict about her way of life than she admits. Why else would she have gotten so emotional during our discussion of the Oneida community? My jealousy began to subside even as I realized that Sigmund was right – she is a fascinating woman.

"Loyalty to one man is spiritual slavery, Margaret," Lou said to me. "Remember that."

"Yes, well . . ." I trailed off, once again not sure how to respond. Sigmund stood and announced that we must be off. He had patients to see this afternoon, and the appointed time was quickly approaching.

We talked very little on the way home. I pondered the meaning of her last comment, directed solely to me. Lou admitted that she is fascinated by love, so intrigued and so mystified that she is writing a paper on the subject, attributing its power to the novelty of each new person. I cannot help admiring her courage, and her words will stay with me. Yet I wonder if the way she keeps it all intellectual – she wonders about love and so she decides to write a paper about it – really comes from a fear of letting go, of surrendering herself to the most powerful emotion. Has she ever given herself fully? As fully as I have given myself to Sigmund? Perhaps in her very emancipation she has been cheated.

Has Lou Andreas-Salome known such power, to set apart one great love from all of her many affairs? I doubt it, and yet, as she looked at me, I saw pity in her eyes. To her, I must appear so drab, dependent, and uncreative. In a way, she is right. To the outer world, my life lacks color. My secret must remain. Sigmund knows differently, and this must sustain me.

Still, I wonder how much he understands. My help with his work – it is more than just translations – is vitally important at this point in his career. On his own, he lacks the sight to break forward in his field of research. With me at his side, the work appears limitless, with the answers ultimately within reach.

*March 2, 1897*

This morning after breakfast, Sigmund called me into his study. We hadn't spoken much since the luncheon yesterday, although I have been thinking of nothing else. What a fascinating woman Lou really is.

The room felt cool, and it took a moment for my eyes to adjust to the darkness. A soft spring breeze wafted in from the open window.

Sigmund appeared serious, so I sat rather nervously in the armchair across from him at his desk. I couldn't imagine what was wrong. "You know, Minna, I was rather surprised at how quiet you were during yesterday's luncheon. Didn't you enjoy yourself?"

"Oh yes, Sigi. It was very enjoyable. In fact, I haven't been able to stop thinking about what was said."

"Well," he paused, "it doesn't do for a woman to be overly aggressive, Minna, but there is no need to hide in the corner like a little mouse either!"

I felt as though he had slapped me. "Is that what you think of me?" I demanded angrily, the blood rising to my face. "Am I your trained monkey – to perform for your friends?"

"Now, Minna," he said, trying to calm me, but I would not let him continue.

"You cannot expect me to be witty and charming when the woman could not even make an effort to remember my name. To her I was just an extra person in the audience. She had no interest in me. She was bent on impressing you and Arthur, and you have certainly never made me a part of conversations you have held with Arthur in the past! Am I suddenly allowed out into the public to show what I have been working on with you? Is that what you want now, Sigmund?" I had never been so angry with him. I was clenching my hands in an effort to stop them from shaking.

"Minna, dear, I am simply trying to help you improve yourself. We must all learn how to hold ourselves in social situations."

"I don't need your training, Sigmund," I said in a very low, firm voice. "I am capable of relating to persons on my own – they are interested in *me*. Not only as an appendage to you!" With this, I turned and left his study, slamming the door behind me. I ran to my room, passing a bewildered Marty in the hallway.

Now, hours later, I am realizing that Sigmund has begun to stifle my own nature. This very nature that I had hidden for so many years has again risen to the surface. I must still love him, and want to be with him, but no longer can I do his very bidding just because of who he is. He will have to accept *me* — the person that I am! Perhaps a period of separation is necessary. I have no outside friends or interests. I must attempt to extend myself in a more outward manner — and then he will see that I can conduct myself properly in social matters.

I am so hurt! I never would have believed that he thought so little of me!

## March 12, 1897

Sigmund and I have allowed our tempers to cool, although we have not been together for more than a week. I am no longer quite so blinded by my affection. He is, after all, only a man. One that I love, perhaps, but still mortal.

Martha asked me if Sigi and I had disagreed. Though I long to confide in someone, I cannot tell her the truth. I explained that we had simply had a difference of opinion on some of his work, and she seemed to accept this.

Anna has become a great comfort. She is a delight to play with and has begun to imitate words just like a little parrot. She adores playing in the courtyard with a large ball, always sure that the next time she will catch it.

I can only confide here, in my diary. I feel so terribly alone.

## March 27, 1897

Sigmund has taken on a new patient, a young man named Wilhelm. I gather that he is a medical student from the textbooks he was carrying when he arrived for his first appointment.

He is tall and slender, with brown hair and soft brown eyes. I was very taken with his gentle manner and his warm, friendly smile. He was several minutes early for his appointment, so to pass the time, we chatted and eventually wound up discussing some poetry he was writing. He blushed when I told him sincerely that I would like to see some of his work. I must say I believe I blushed too. It is foolish, but I feel a bit like a schoolgirl with a crush.

In general, I do not discuss the patients with Sigmund. He maintains a high standard of confidentiality. This evening, however, I mustered enough courage to turn idle conversation to Wilhelm.

We were, as usual, playing a game of tarok. Sigmund was enjoying himself, and he was the most relaxed with me that I have seen since our disagreement.

"Your newest patient, Wilhelm, seems to be a very interesting man, Sigi," I said softly, pretending to concentrate on the cards.

"Yes, he is a most thoughtful man," he responded. "It is a pity he is not relating well with his wife. I've found that a wife's support is so important for a man's success."

I ignored the remark, although under other circumstances I might take offense. Obviously, Sigmund was deep in thought about the game and was not guarding his tongue as he might usually. I proceeded with my questioning.

"It is only for marital matters, then, that he is seeing you?"

Sigmund looked up with a frown creasing his brow. "You know I cannot discuss cases with you, Minna. I am sworn to confidentiality. Why are you so interested in Wilhelm?"

Startled, I said that he reminded me of my brother. Sigmund told me not to become too attached as he did not think the sessions would continue for a long period of time.

Another married man, then. Will I never find a man free to love me, as I am capable of loving? Am I doomed to love those tied to other women?

## March 31, 1897

Wilhelm came again on Tuesday, but Sigmund was ready to see him at once and so he and I barely had a chance to speak. How disappointed I was! But today he more than made up for it. When he arrived for this afternoon's appointment with Sigi, he presented me with a great bunch of white gladiolus. I blushed with pleasure and left him in the waiting area while I fetched a vase. While I was gone, Sigi took him into the consulting room for the session.

I brought one of Sigi's manuscripts that I had been reading for errors to the waiting area and began to work halfheartedly on it, hoping for a glimpse of Wilhelm when he left. The gladiolus were proudly displayed on the tabletop beside my chair. I inhaled their luscious fragrance with every breath.

I was startled when Sigi opened the door to the consulting room to usher Wilhelm out. "Oh, Minna! Just the person I wanted to see! Would you come to my study to discuss some correspondence?" he asked.

"Of course, Sigmund," I answered, busily gathering up the

manuscript that had been spread open in my lap. I noticed that Wilhelm seemed to be delaying leaving, fumbling with his hat. He sidled up to me shyly and asked in a tender voice, so soft that Sigmund could not hear in the next room, to join him for coffee tomorrow afternoon. I accepted quickly and am waiting with excited apprehension.

I have an odd feeling that I should tell Sigi about my appointment or even ask his permission, but this is ridiculous. Here I am, almost thirty-two years old, and I find that I am treating Sigmund as if he were my father. What an odious role to put my lover in!

## April 1, 1897

I am feeling very high-spirited tonight. Coffee with Wilhelm provided great pleasure. I left without telling anyone where I would be and met him at the Café Merkur, which of course reminded me of the luncheon with Arthur Schnitzler and Lou Andreas-Salome. I regaled Wilhelm with bits of dialogue from the luncheon and gossip about Frau Lou's life.

"She sounds like quite a woman!" he remarked, and I realized that I agreed with him. Then Wilhelm and I talked a bit about our childhoods. He has been to Hamburg only once and was very interested to hear more about Wandsbeck and Hamburg, the museums, the Reeperbahm, and the tawdry Saint Pauli district.

I found myself remembering details of Hamburg and my childhood I would never have known were in my head. I recalled the colors of the lakes, the shapes of the many ships at the port, the sounds and smells of vendors at the markets, and it was challenging but exhilarating trying to fit them all into slippery words.

Wilhelm told me a little bit about his childhood as well and about his marriage. Apparently his wife, like Marty and myself, is from a Jewish family without much money. When she married a medical student, she believed her ship had come in, but since, according to Wilhelm, she has been whining and nagging. During their courtship, she was charmed by the love poetry he wrote, but now she rails at him, calling his poetry a waste of time and his artistic tendencies a form of laziness. Wilhelm talked about his wife very lightly, almost jokingly, but I could tell the discordance hurt him deeply.

I have moved the beautiful white gladiolus from the waiting area to my room so that I may enjoy them every waking moment I am in the room.

When he walked me back to 19 Bergasse, he kissed my hand and said, "I brought the flowers because they reminded me of you, Minna; tall and graceful yet with buds of plump sensuality and fair, delicate white skin."

## April 4, 1897

I took the children to the Prater this afternoon while Martha and Sigmund had lunch with Amalie. Sigmund grumbles so about this weekly luncheon that you would think it wasn't his own mother.

The children enjoyed the warm spring air, and we all were amazed at the hundreds of different colors of tulips growing in the flower beds. They ran and tumbled all afternoon until, full of ice cream, we stumbled wearily back home.

I find that I am enjoying the outside world more every day. Although I do still love Sigmund deeply, there is an attraction to looking into the outside world. Somehow I feel a bit wicked about my coffee date with Wilhelm.

## April 5, 1897

I have just finished penning a note to Wilhelm stating that I must not see him again in the future. The warm blush of romance has been frozen in my heart. How could I have been so foolish to think that Sigmund would not be hurt? I have betrayed the man I love — and it must never happen again.

Sigmund was alone in his study late last night. Although our relationship has seemed to change, our work together has not. I have been trying to instill in him the idea that love of one's self is most important and that before treating anyone he must place himself inside that person to see what he or she needs to feel self-love.

He was strangely oppressed, quiet, and solemn. Sigi spoke in short, precise sentences and never dealt with anything beyond the surface of our conversation. I was uncomfortable, aware that something had gone awry — so I hesitatingly asked him.

"Sigmund," I said, pulling my chair closer to him, "what is this distance between us? What have I done to make you withdraw from me?"

The grief in his eyes was so intense that I could feel its pain tear at my heart. He sat motionless for several moments and then, to my shock, began to cry. Soft, quiet sobs shook his body. I embraced him tightly and pulled him down into my lap, his face pressed against my bosom.

"I cannot ask it of you, Minna," he moaned. "I have no right to keep you from other men." He abruptly pulled away and with his back turned to me wiped his face with a large white handkerchief. "Forgive me," he said in a strong voice. "I don't know what came over me." He pulled a book randomly from a shelf and began to flip through it. I knew he was trying to regain his composure.

I spoke softly and continuously for more than an hour, trying to explain my actions. In the end, we did reach an understanding, and if anything, I believe this episode has strengthened our commitment to each other. But I know that I must never again hurt him. He has suffered so from the criticism of his work and the blocks he has reached in his career — I cannot hurt him further.

How could I have been so stupid? So unthinking and thoughtless? Never again will I let someone's flattery turn my head.

## April 12, 1897

Martin is once again ill with a throat infection. He had a very high fever during the night. Martha and Josephine took turns nursing him all night long. The poor boy alternated between shivering so much as to shake the bed to throwing off all the bedclothes and soaking the sheets with perspiration. Today, the fever had broken, and he was simply weak and pale.

Sophie collected a small fistful of flowers that we placed ceremoniously on the bedside table. I am certain that Martin will bounce back within a few days, yet the frequency of his throat infections is troubling.

## April 16, 1897

In less than one month, we will again journey to Aussee. Sigmund has been working feverishly on his dream book, hoping to have enough completed to show to Wilhelm. It is planned that the Fliess family will visit us for several days, and a neighboring guest house has been reserved for them.

I have been busy with a project of my own – although under Sigmund's direction, of course. It occurred to me, and he agreed, that it would be worthwhile to study the children to confirm his ideas about childhood sexuality. Martha would disapprove, so she is not to know. I will merely begin spending more time with the children and helping Josephine with the care. I believe that this will bring me closer to Annerl. She has been drawing further away as she grows older. No longer is she content to follow me around like a shadow. She is very independent, quick to temper, and appears to already have a strong will of her own. I have hoped that she would emulate my ways rather than those of her mother. She appears to have chosen neither of us – and is striking out on her own at the wise old age of less than two. Even Josephine finds her difficult – incorrigible, she says, although with a good deal of fondness. Sigmund only smiles at her antics, and Anna tries very hard to please him.

I am to look for things that could be heard in infancy or early childhood that could not be understood until later and that might be misinterpreted. Also, Sigmund suggested watching for the buildup of mental forces that might later impede the course of sexual instinct and restrict its flow, such as disgust, shame, or imposed aesthetic or moral "ideals."

I find this type of work fascinating and stimulating. Sigmund and I work so well together. Frequently, it is as though our minds have merged into one – and neither is sure from whom the initial idea came.

Sigmund has made good progress on his dream book. He says that he gained insight from the time when we practiced the witches' ceremonies.

We were sitting together, as was our practice late at night in his study. The entire household was sleeping so the usual thumping from above had ceased. Only the street noises drifted in through the open window. As frequently happened, the discussion became "otherworldly," as if all time had stopped while we intellectualized an idea or question.

Sigmund was unusually affectionate, and I sat on his lap, resting my head against his shoulder. "We experienced another consciousness during the witchcraft ceremonies. Perhaps dreams can be seen in that light – as another land with its own rule and markers," I mused aloud.

Sigi followed my thoughts closely, as he frequently did, without further explanation. "Yes." He seemed pleased with the image. "When the outside censor is weakened through sleep, we can enter the land – the Via Regia to the unconscious."

"And once there," I continued on slowly, rubbing and intertwining his fingers with mine, "the early wishes, the ideas held in chains, the deepest needs can be expressed in dreams. But why then aren't the dreams clearer?"

He had closed his eyes, drifting along with the chain of conversation. With my question his lids flew open and he spoke with the energy that I loved to hear.

"*Traumenstellung* – the distortions come to play to disguise the dream, to make it more acceptable to our waking consciousness," he said with certainty. "This dream work, the *traumarbeit*, is a shield, but we can go around it by following the train of associations and images and thus bring the dream into the light of day."

I left his lap and moved across to my own chair. He resisted my leaving him but retained my hand in his and gave it a resounding kiss. "So we are the conquistadors of the dream," I laughed. "Are you Don Quixote," I added, "and I your faithful Sancho Panza?"

"I'll be your Don Quixote, Minna, but if I am only battling with mirrors, I will reflect only narcissism and if the enemy is but windmills . . ." His voice trailed off.

"They do flail, and Krafft-Ebing might look like a windmill," I said playfully.

We embraced again and sat for a long while just enjoying the sense of being. The stillness of the night echoed the peacefulness in my heart. How I long to openly show my affection for Sigi to the world. He is such a brilliant man.

## May 5, 1897

Sigmund was again discussing his dream book. The work is slow, but he is enjoying it a great deal. Tonight, he spoke about dreams as a parable about a comedy at the opera house. The audience is usually quiet, paying rapt attention to the production, but what if some ill-bred individual was disturbing everybody in his vicinity through talking, laughing, stomping his feet, and in all other ways being disagreeable. We would not be surprised if several strong men came to eject this disturbing intruder from the opera hall. He is now in the position of a repressed thought. Now, if the strong men who had ejected him lock the door and place their chairs in front of it, they are acting in the manner of a resistance to keep up the repression. The inside of the opera house is then analogous to the consciousness and the outside analogous to the unconscious. The intruder, finding himself on the outside in the middle of the Kartnerstrasse, would be angry and might become belligerent, calling from the outside, banging on the door, and in all possible ways making his presence still known.

This is analogous to what happens with dreams. The unconscious, the repressed thoughts, still make their noise, and when the disturbance becomes more than those inside the opera house can tolerate, when the intruder interferes with the normal enjoyment, we then have a symptom. In dream analysis, one must go through the dream and find out more about the intruder, why he is creating such a ruckus, and perhaps allow him to reenter, providing that he is no longer rowdy.

Martha is irritated that I have been so busy with Sigmund's work and have not been able to help with preparations for our travel. She has turned down his invitation to attend the Burgtheatre performance of *The*

*Master of Palmyra.* I hope she is not going to become bitter like Mama. Although we do not have a great deal in common, life would be very unpleasant if she were to sour.

## May 10, 1897

The play did not disappoint us – I was kept enthralled by the masterpiece for the full four hours. It started with an early Christian wanderer, a young girl named Zoe, who was trying to spread the word of Christianity to the Zeus-worshiping pagans of Palmyra. Eventually, she martyrs herself, and in the second act, she appears in a new incarnation as Phoebe, a spoiled, superficial, but captivating Roman woman. Sigi kept nudging me, whispering when he thought a detail in the play was not accurate, but I was content to enjoy the story line without his constant demand for authenticity. In the third act, Zoe's reincarnation is as Persida, a deeply religious mother and housekeeper. Then there is one act where she plays an attractive, naive young boy; finally, in the last act, she is Zenobia, blending the qualities of all four together, including lightness, charm, seriousness, compassion, and wisdom.

Sigmund said he was fascinated by the changing character of the woman and likened it to psychology on a stage – all the elements of the woman's personality were separated then combined at the end into the one very beautiful person.

I found the pressing crowd, moving forward together toward the brightly lit lobby of the Burg, to be oppressive. The perfume of women mingled with the bright lights and the loud voices were too much to experience after the beauty of the play, and I begged Sigmund to take me outside.

We moved away from the entrance and down the path before we were able to be free from the people spilling forth. Together, we turned around for a moment and looked back through the gardens at the Grand Burg and over across the Ringstrasse to the park where new electric lighting made the towers of the Rathaus glow eerily. From the path, the Burgtheatre looked like some kind of medieval castle, with the great tower sticking up behind it. Sigi and I walked slowly through the Volksgarten, touching hands, and I was afraid to break the silence.

"An amazing, remarkable work," Sigmund finally said softly. "And did you notice, Minna, that in the first act when Zoe prayed to the Spirit of Life, the Spirit of Death appeared, uninvited, at the same time? With every life force comes the death force."

I continued along with the same thoughts. "Then Apellee made a bargain for eternal life despite the warnings of the Spirit of Life that 'Life without end can be regret without end.' So that Life, when denied its counterpart, Death, must imitate it—become a kind of a living death."

"Yes, Minna! The moral there is completeness, a warning against isolating what may appear to be the 'good' part of something and neglecting its other aspects. Then when Apellee cannot have death, he seeks the next best—forgetfulness. This is exactly what my patients with hysteria do! They cannot die from an unpleasant memory but they try to forget, to drown the memory. Death's equivalent — repression — *Verdrangung*."

We emerged from the garden and walked back out onto the Ringstrasse. At night this was a gathering place for enormous numbers of prostitutes. I usually avoided it, but tonight Sigi and I found ourselves in their midst.

Vienna has grown used to their presence and even provides each woman with an identification card, showing that she is under medical surveillance. "Hand arbeiterin, or hand workers" they are called, an odd euphemism which is the butt of many jokes in the city.

As Sigi and I walked up the street, it was easy to tell the classes of prostitutes apart. The very richest, the "coquettes," dallied in the garden we had just walked through or stayed inside the Kursalon or near the Imperial Hotel or the Bristol. The cheaper ones stood outside the dance halls and taverns of the Prater, and the cheapest of all walked around outside night shelters or slept under the bridges. The women were of all ages, all shapes, all races, and I had heard whispering of special houses that catered to fetishists as well. Feeling bold, I asked Sigmund about such houses.

He looked at me with amusement but did answer. "Yes, they cater to all kinds of bizarre tastes, with spy holes, mirrors, and even women dressed in the costumes of nuns, schoolgirls, or anything a man might request, so long as he has the gulden."

"What sort of men go to those places? Do most men?" I was horrified but curious. For all of my research with Sigmund into sexuality, I was terribly inexperienced. I wanted to ask him if he had ever been to a brothel but choked back the question.

"As long as a society demands that betrothals be so long, for many men there can be no other outlet for years," Sigi replied seriously. "Only a select few are capable of sublimating this drive into creative or scientific work, and even that is not wholly successful."

"Are you thinking of yourself, Sigi?" I asked playfully as he took my arm.

"Well, yes," he said hesitantly, "but there are many others as well. Self-gratification leads to neurasthenia, and for many men the problem continues even when they are married. Excessive 'coitus interruptus' causes mental symptoms as well. Do you remember when Frau Lou said that lack of a good contraceptive was responsible for social repression of sexual urges more than any other factor?"

I nodded, remembering back to our argument and blushing with shame.

"I believe she is right because fear of pregnancy can make an otherwise responsive wife frigid, and that, too, will drive men to the brothels."

We were passing the parliament building and saw several well-dressed young women haggling over price with a young man.

"And the women," I asked timidly. "Do they do what is asked — even perversions?"

He walked silently for several minutes before responding. "Minna, we live in a strange world. The use of the mouth as a sexual organ is regarded as a perversion if the lips or tongue are brought to the genitals of the other. Yet we find it entirely normal if the lips of one are brought to the lips and tongue of the other — which we call kissing. Thus, the definition of normal is simply the point of contact."

We passed a tall, well-lit building on the right-hand side of the street adorned with statues on the top ledges just as a handsomely dressed man in a dark suit hurried out of it alone.

"It is just a rumor, Minna, but I have heard that this is the house for foot fetishists, for men who love feet and shoes," Sigi whispered to me, the sparkle back in his eyes. "Supposedly, men go in there and buy a shoe from one of the women and get as much pleasure from stroking the shoe as he might from the full act with the woman."

"So a fetishist is someone who mistakes one part for the whole?" I asked.

"Yes, that might be a good way of describing it," Sigi said thoughtfully. "It is an overvaluation, perhaps similar to the statues or fetishes that some savages believe embody their gods. Yet the situation only becomes abnormal when the fetish becomes so necessary that it actually takes the place of the normal object — like the man with the shoe."

"But how would such a perversion develop?" I asked as we continued walking.

"An interesting question, Minna. No doubt, it develops in much the same way as most other neurotic conditions. There could be the same sort of pattern of normal desire that was punished or repressed, then the energy is transferred onto a chance object or activity. A little boy trying to see his big sister naked is very likely to be punished but a little boy playing with a shoe is far less likely to arouse suspicion."

"And a mother's shoe is certainly what a little child sees," I said, "so patterns may be set at a very young age?"

"Yes. The child does indeed focus on his mother's shoe," he observed. "Patterns must result from childhood sexuality. A great many adult women find the thoughts of sex disgusting, yet it appears that there is an age, very early in childhood, when there is no disgust or distaste associated with any of the bodily parts or functions. We need to try to find out at what age, and through what process, the negative reactions are learned."

By now we were strolling down the Bergasse, and as we approached the large wooden door of the entranceway, Sigmund removed his timepiece from his vest pocket and held it in such a way that it reflected the nearby gaslight. "Nearly two A.M." he said. "It must have been close to midnight when the play let out, and we got so involved in talking that we barely noticed the passage of time." Poor Marty, with her headache. I felt badly that I had not thought of her all evening. We entered the flat quietly, moving as two cats might through the darkened rooms. Before retiring, Sigi kissed me with a hard, burning kiss that lingered on my lips. As I pulled off my gown and corset to change into my nightdress, I caught sight of my figure in the mirror. I thought of how Sigmund had looked at me earlier at the theatre, how his eyes roamed approvingly over my body. Very discreetly, of course, most gentlemanly. I'm sure he thought I did not notice, but a woman always knows, I think, when she is being observed – and desired. With my corset off, I turned and twisted to see the way I looked. Yes, my breasts are large and full but not yet sagging badly. I worry that I am perhaps too plump, but my frame is large. My dark hair when it hangs down serves as a soft frame for my face.

I am no beauty but am attractive enough to men. I blush to think of myself so objectively. This is something I have not done since I was a young girl just developing.

Ignaz, too, had found me attractive. Really, not since that time with him have I felt so much a woman. I am no longer afraid to show my femininity. Sigmund's attention has aroused within me another whole element of my being - and I like it.

## May 13, 1897

Although the day was kept busy with Martha preparing for the travel to Bad Aussee, I slipped away with Sigi tonight to the Grienstaeidl Café at Arthur's invitation. Sigi left his work gladly, saying, "Everything is seething within me. I am awaiting the next surge of ideas, and they have not come."

As we walked through the fresh night air, he told me that he is greatly looking forward to seeing his dearest friend. While I feel privileged to be somewhat of a confidante, I know that he holds his deepest feelings and thoughts in reserve for his conversations with Wilhelm. I do not begrudge him this, feeling only pleasure that he is fortunate to have such a close friend.

The lights from the café lit up the dark sidewalk in warm, beckoning pools. We entered and located Arthur, who was holding court in the far corner. He greeted us then casually asked Sigmund how life was at the university and whether his appointment as Professor Extraordinarius was forthcoming. I was surprised by Arthur's insensitivity. How could he forget that Sigi has been ostracized ever since the lecture on hysteria last year? Perhaps he was spoiled by having a father who was not only a professor of medicine but a leader in the development of the medical school.

Sigmund remained silent at Arthur's question, but Theodor Herzl, who was sitting at a nearby table, answered for him. "Arthur, you know that is no simple question. Sigmund is a scholar, a luminary, and a *Jew*. In France, Captain Alfred Dreyfus has been publicly shamed in a kangaroo court and our government says nothing, even though Esterhazy was part of the whole frame-up. Our leaders order that Jewish schoolchildren must sit on separate benches in school. The forces of power here in Vienna are tied to the same anti-Semitic movement, and from such people you expect fairness and honor, such as a university appointment or advancement? Bah!" he ended in a disgusted tone of voice.

"You, Theodor, see everything as anti-Semitism," Arthur countered good-naturedly.

"I see what is there," Herzl said with force, his large body shaking with emotion. Swiveling in his chair to face Sigmund, he continued while gesturing wildly with his hands, "If you need proof, just look at Karl Lueger's mayoral platform. He blames all the poor conditions in the city on Jews, and where do you expect that kind of hatred-fueling power can end? There is no answer but the creation of a separate Jewish state with Jewish universities. Arthur," he continued, "your concern with love affairs, trysts, and manners with dashes of psychology added in are blinding you."

Sigmund's face was red, and he looked uncomfortable. "I do not believe this is the proper forum to debate my university career," he said indignantly. "Let us proceed to other topics of conversation." He spoke softly but with such force that I could tell he was growing angry.

Arthur was silent for a moment, appearing somewhat puzzled at the turn of events. Herzl sat heavily in his chair, shaking his head with an air of doom and despair.

I groped for some safe area of conversation, unable to bear the strained silence. "How is your new publication, *Die Welt*, progressing, Herr Herzl?"

He leapt enthusiastically onto the new topic, and Sigmund sank down, with a grateful glance at me, onto a nearby chair. I joined him at the table and motioned for the waiter as Herzl was talking. "*Die Welt* will become the voice of Zionism. It will broadcast the real danger so that everyone can finally see it," he announced proudly. "But we need more writers and leaders."

"And the convention?" asked Sigmund.

"We've had problems with the first Zionist convention. I desired to hold it in Munich but had to change to Basel in August. The rabbis are against it, you know, and everyone is afraid of alienating the Rothschilds. The banking Jews don't want any change — not if there is any risk to their money," he finished fervently.

We listened politely, sipping on the hot coffee, but Herzl's single-mindedness, his obvious obsession, troubled me as it never had before. Poor man. He is so bright, and yet he tunnels all of his ideas into that one direction and is so convinced that he is right that it is almost impossible to talk with him. In a sudden flash, I realized that some people must perceive Sigmund in this same way.

Yet there is truth in what Herzl was saying. Sigi mentioned to me afterward that in a recent letter from Wilhelm Fliess, he was upset that his own children had been forced to sit apart from the Gentiles in school. Anti-Semitism is real enough, as we know only too well, and I'm sure Herzl is right, too, if only because along with everything else the university holds against Sigi, being a Jew can only make things worse. Imagine them considering a Jew who talks openly about sex.

## May 17, 1897

A slight change in our travel plans. It has been arranged that I will take the children to Bad Aussee and will be joined by Marty and Sigi shortly after Whitsun.

Marty explained to me after dinner that she wants a little time with Sigmund alone – without the children. She was obviously nervous and would not look me in the eye. I perceived a trace of color in her face as she spoke. Was she trying to reestablish her marital relationship???

While my intellect tells me that I have no claim to Sigmund, my heart beats with wild indignation. Once again, I am relegated to the position of the spinster aunt who will care for the children. Worst of all, Sigmund did not say a word.

## May 23, 1897

Tomorrow I leave for Aussee. I am determined to make the best of the situation. Sigmund's expression has become so drawn that I cannot bring myself to cause him any further distress.

This evening, after the children had been excused from the dinner table, Sigi said painfully, "Maybe I shouldn't care so much about recognition, but it is not only myself I am thinking of. My practice would grow and the whole family would benefit."

Martha answered him softly, "Wait until after the vote has been taken before you get upset. Perhaps things will come out in our favor – if there is any justice in the world."

"If there is any justice in the world," Sigi gloomily repeated after her. I remained silent, collecting the dishes from around the table. I have been part of too many conversations about Sigi's appointment. After all this while, I, too, have become discouraged. I must be careful not to allow his black moods to become contagious.

Marty, however, seemed to be cheerful and at peace tonight. She had been humming before dinner, arranging her favorite orchids in a vase as a centerpiece for the table, and now gazed serenely back at Sigi. "The vote will come in three weeks?"

"Yes. I did not know you were following this so closely, Martha," he said with surprise, "and then I will be able to see my enemies more clearly, in the open! That is, if they have the courage to come out and show their faces instead of hiding like vermin in crevices," he concluded vehemently.

Marty was silent for a moment, arranging and rearranging the silverware on the table in front of her. "Just remember that your family knows who you are. We don't need a university appointment to tell us."

Sigi nodded without speaking, but I could tell he was deeply touched. I quietly went into the kitchen, feeling somehow out of place, almost like an intruder. Martha seems to be improving, no longer lost in that melancholy world.

In any case, I must not be upset. Sigmund will need all the help and support he can get from all of us for the next few weeks, and possibly after the vote as well. If Martha is able to help him, I must step back. I love him so much and only want to see him strong once again.

## June 12, 1897

We received a rare telegram today from Sigmund. It read:

*Vote was 22 to 10 in favor of appointment. STOP.*
*Celebration is in order. STOP.*
*Will arrive in Aussee with Martha on June 20. STOP.*

The older children were excited to hear the news. The thought of their papa being appointed Professor Extraordinarius was thrilling. Even the little ones caught the cheerful mood, and we all joined hands and danced a little jig.

Later in the day, however, when I had time to think more about the appointment, a nagging fear began to grow in the back of my mind. The vote was only the first step. Now he must be officially appointed.

Please don't let him be disappointed this time. He is such a good man, and I love him so.

## June 18, 1897

The days have passed quickly. As Josephine is with us, I have had much time to become rested and refreshed. While I miss Sigmund desperately, I no longer feel angry at our separation. Once again, I have learned that I simply must accept our unusual relationship as it is – and not expect it to extend beyond its confined boundaries.

The children have become used to a routine of walks, swims, picnics, and mushroom hunting. They are all tanned brown as berries. Even little Anna has begun to splash in the lake. Ernst hopes to impress his father with the number of species of mushrooms he can identify.

Much must be done to prepare for their arrival. Sigmund's writing office has been set up as last year. I have again furnished it sparsely – hoping that the simplicity will soothe his troubled mind.

## June 21, 1897

Marty and Sigmund arrived late yesterday afternoon. I could see instantly that Sigi was tense and worried. They were both happy to be reunited with their family and were covered with children from the moment they alighted from the carriage. The chaos and excitement continued throughout the evening. At one point, when we were preparing dinner, Martha began to confide that Dr. Nothnagel came to visit shortly before they left Vienna, but we were interrupted time and time again by the demands of the children. She simply ended her attempt to finish by saying, "You must speak with Sigmund. He needs to talk."

Finally, the children were put to bed and Josephine and Martha retired to their rooms. I made a pretense of staying awake to straighten the kitchen so that I could talk privately with Sigmund. I rapped softly on his office door and opened it slowly. He was seated by the window, staring off into the night sky. "Come in, Minna dear," he said.

I was startled by his dejected appearance and knew in my heart that my worst fears were confirmed. He had not received the appointment after all. After a gentle embrace, he began to speak in a slow but steady voice.

"Dr. Nothnagel, chairman of the department of internal medicine at the University of Vienna Medical School, came to see me several days before our journey here." Sigi ran his finger across the golden wood grain on his desk's top, following its swirls and lines. Finally, he looked up at me, and I yearned to reach out and smooth the tired, discouraged lines from his face. "Nothnagel is a fine man. As a professor of medicine, he is so dedicated that he is at the hospital more than twelve hours a day, working with his students and his patients. His presence was an honor. Unfortunately, his visit was motivated by frustration and disgust."

I waited expectantly for him to continue.

"I was naive and saw the situation as I wanted it to be. Von Hartel is going to overturn the favorable recommendation of the committee of six nominating professors and the majority vote of the faculty. It is more complicated than I had realized, and he is not acting alone."

"Who is against it then, and why?" I asked defiantly. "Is it the emperor?"

"No, Minna." Sigmund laughed with an ugly, sarcastic sound. "The emperor Franz Josef stays the emperor because he knows enough to keep out of political business in Vienna. He has discovered that secret of survival — as I might do well to emulate," Sigi added. "Franz Josef's strength is only in his name. He is sequestered away in the Schonbrunn palace with Katherine Schratt while the empress Elizabeth is on the island of Corfu ill with prolonged grief over Crown Prince Rudolf's suicide. Our 'leaders' are safely out of the way."

"Then who is against you?" I persisted, afraid of the answer. A large white moth fluttered in through the open window. I watched it dance to its death in the candlelight.

"Minna, I should have known. I knew, but I let myself forget. Do you remember last summer when I told you about my conversation with Nothnagel? I didn't listen to him. He warned me that Baron von Krafft-Ebing could not let me succeed. My theories challenge his own theories, and he must protect himself. His *Psychopathia Sexualis* has been the authority on the subject since 1886, and he says that sexual perversions do not come from any factor in childhood but from constitution alone. He has testified to that before the courts in criminal cases."

"And he would destroy your career — your reputation — just to protect his theory?" I was filled with loathing for this ruthless man.

Sigi nodded silently. "He is sly. Krafft-Ebing and Nothnagel proposed me for the post jointly. Krafft-Ebing's recommendation was lukewarm, but he still appeared to be my supporter. Yet he is secretive and malicious. Nothnagel said that after Krafft-Ebing recommended me, he went to the minister of education and used his rank and influence with the aristocracy to get his way." Sigi said with anger, "He keeps a smile on his face while knifing me in the back!"

"Is Dr. Nothnagel truly supportive of you?" I asked apprehensively.

"He claims to be. Yes, I think he is, Minna. Nothnagel is an honest man, and he is deeply troubled by Krafft-Ebing's tactics, yet he told me he is powerless. Of course, von Hartel must have his own personal stake in this somewhere or else why could he have been manipulated so easily by Krafft-Ebing? Yet no one outside of this little political circle would believe this story." He slouched down wearily in his chair. "Minna, once again I feel so bitter."

"You were betrayed," I said softly, yearning to comfort him.

"I do not know what to do," he said with utter despair.

For the first time, I took the initiative and placed a pillow on the floor. Then, although my heart was pounding, I turned toward him and held out my hands. He rose from his chair and we embraced passionately. As we sank down onto the floor together, I knew only that Sigmund needed my love in his defeat.

## July 1, 1897

Sigmund is even deeper into one of his black moods. We had been planning for Wilhelm Fleiss and his family to visit during our time here at Aussee. Unfortunately, the schedule became much too complicated, what with other stops they had to make along the way, and ultimately their stay with us has been cancelled. I know how important this visit was to Sigmund. Although he talks freely to me of his feelings, he needs another man, a close friend such as Wilhelm, to listen and share his thoughts.

Martha and Josephine are caring almost entirely for the children these days, except when I slip in to observe their sexual explorations. Sigmund has been giving me hours and hours of work, proofreading his manuscripts and poring over patient records.

It appears that Martha and Sigmund were not able to recapture the passion of their marriage in their time alone. Martha has not discussed it with me, and I have not asked, but he has come to me every night since they arrived in Aussee. I glory in his passion. This is truly the meaning of being a woman.

## July 3, 1897

I have been having nightmares about guilt and rejection. In last night's dream, I was alone on a train. Somehow everything seemed sinister, even the conductor who took my ticket. I kept asking him where the train was going.

"Marriage," he said, "between two." Finally the train came to a stop and I got out with my bags, but the station wasn't there. It wasn't deserted, just not there! Everything was empty. I was alone. I awoke drenched with perspiration, although the night air was cool and sweet.

The meaning of the dream is clear enough to me. I am frightened of losing Sigi, but I know there has to be more.

## July 4, 1897

The specter of the nightmare continued to haunt me until I asked Sigmund for his interpretation. Under his direction, I relaxed my mind and allowed the associations, the pictures, to come. I began as a railway traveler . . . from the train . . . the station. The Hamburg station, home with Mama, domineering, forcing me to go. Feelings of being controlled and feelings of anger. Mama in charge, conducting me away from Ignaz, alone, empty. No, Mama won't conduct me away from Sigmund, I thought angrily, rapidly returning to full awareness. Sigi was observing my struggle with such love and empathy that tears sprang to my eyes. He took me onto his lap and told me of a dream that almost seemed to answer mine. "I was walking up the stairs very briskly, with no clothing on, when suddenly I noticed that a naked, large-breasted woman was coming up behind me. I became rooted to the spot, unable to move, overcome by that paralysis that occurs in dreams." He paused and I urged him to continue while snuggling deeper into his shoulder.

"My associations led to fear. You see, I was turning my back to the woman, going away. She was alluring, but I could not move, could not take her into my arms. I was so paralyzed by conflict that I couldn't show her my love. Yet what I remember of the dream has been disfigured – as memory reproduces only a fragment of the dream, and even the insignificant features can be important in analysis. The stairway I associated with my ambition and the fear that my career is paralyzed. The woman, looking like you, Minna dear, is my love, and yet also she represents all of my loves: my love of conquest, fame, money – all symbolized by you – and the fear that I cannot have them. There was more, but I could not continue as a resistance impeded the free-flow association. Somehow, though, I know it is guilt. Simply guilt." He kissed me lightly on the top of my head and held me tightly.

After a long silence, I said, "We must go away. We need to be together without having to worry so much about being discovered."

Sigi's dark eyes brightened as thought took form. "Yes, we must. Especially now. Minna, I am going through the worst spell of intellectual paralysis imaginable. Each line I write is torture, and my thoughts are so cloudy that I can't seem to organize them at all."

"Then this is the best time to get away, especially since Wilhelm and his family won't be able to visit," I said firmly. "We could do a walking tour together from Salzburg, then across the Salzach River, and up the valley to Heilbronn. Maybe we could even stay the night at Grodig."

"Perhaps better still, Minna, we could go from Grodig to Untersberg. It is a nice mountain climb, not too difficult but still challenging."

"Good. Let's make the arrangements. When shall we leave?" I asked the question briskly, as if I were a travel broker, and then both of us realized that we would have to explain our travels to Martha.

"What will she say, Sigi?" I asked worriedly.

"Minna," he said rather sadly, "I don't think she would ask many questions. You see, we seem to be growing farther and farther apart, although my love for her is everlasting. I will simply say that I need to research some material and that you must accompany me as my assistant. This will have to satisfy her."

I am so excited that my feet are barely touching the floor. I cannot believe that we will finally be alone together. The prospect of such a trip is so daring!

It is agreed that we will leave on July 15.

## July 10, 1897

Sigmund is eagerly awaiting our trip, as am I. Martha's response was exactly as Sigmund predicted. I can no longer pretend that she doesn't know about us – but it is something that we will never discuss openly. I must learn to live with the guilt and not let it destroy our relationship.

Wilhelm's latest letter to Sigi brought more information about his mathematical figuring. This was to be the beginning of another critical period for Sigmund – a time of intense introspection and understanding. I hope that our travels will enable him to pull his ideas together so that he can again begin with his work.

Sigmund is disturbed by a royalty statement for *Studies in Hysteria*, written with Josef Breuer. Franz Deuticke, his publisher, had printed eight hundred copies, and the selling price is two florins per copy. Sigmund had hoped that they would publish at least fifteen hundred copies. "Franz, this is original work. Every doctor in Austria and Germany will be interested," he had argued, but Deuticke was reluctant to publish even eight hundred. Today's statement was dismal. So far, in two years, the total sale had been only two hundred and fifty copies. With a royalty of less than one-half florin per book to be divided with Josef – it was barely enough to cover the cost of the writing paper. No wonder Sigi feels such discouragement.

I have been reading a book of love poems and stories by the Norwegian author Arne Gaborg. The sensual descriptions fuel my daydreams of passion as I wait for our time alone.

## July 15, 1897

Finally! We arrived in Salzburg on today's afternoon train. Sigmund flagged a two-horse fiacre to the old city and the Hotel Monchsburg – just a block from the Mozarthaus on Getreidegasse. "You know I am indifferent to music," Sigi said as I pointed to Mozart's house. As we passed the main courtyard, strains of a string quartet wafted through the air – the interweaving of the light sounds of violins, violas, and a cello. The beauty of the great fortress of Hohensalzburg was an inspiration to us both.

Sigmund resisted the relaxation at first, but before long, I saw his jaw loosen, and when the wind ruffled his carefully parted hair, he did not reach up to pat it down, as he would have done in Vienna.

From our hotel, we can see the massive castle. It was initially built in 1100 and had many additions built on over the next seven hundred years. It is an incredible monolith, looking like something out of a dark fairy tale.

On the square, vendors selling chestnuts and Burenwurst mingle with the tourists. There are many nuns in white habits and Benedictine monks in flowing brown robes who proceed quietly, seemingly oblivious to the hubbub.

After settling into our hotel (of course, two rooms had been reserved), we toured the beautiful courtyards of the castle. Carved marble statues of the Apostles filled every corner.

"Is this our hiking tour?" Sigmund asked, out of breath and laughing, as we reached the halfway point of our walk to the top of the castle.

"Imagine the people who live at the top, who must go up and down the stairs several times each day! Vienna is a level plain compared to this," I said, panting.

On our way down, we passed through several small narrow streets with shops on either side. Sigmund stopped at one antique store, fascinated by a display of ancient statues depicting mythological creatures. We went in and, after some discussion, he purchased a statue of Aphrodite.

"Minna, what a find," he said appreciatively as he stroked the statue, long-haired and naked with small, well-formed breasts. "The goddess of love and beauty – the one who revered laughter."

"Will she help us laugh more, too?" I asked.

He gathered me close into his arms for an embrace before we continued walking. "She may. The daughter of Zeus is powerful. In Greek legend, she arose from the foam of the sea. The Romans called her Venus." He stopped suddenly in front of another shop. "Stay here," he ordered mischievously. Several minutes later, he reappeared with a small statue of Eros. "Now we have both—mother and son, Aphrodite and Eros. Legend says that Eros can live in man's heart forever unless there is hardness, at which time he departs. Without him . . ."

". . . there is darkness," I completed the sentence.

"Yes," said Sigmund with a mixture of joy and surprise. "You know." He kissed me again, and we laughed together in joy at being alive.

Walking arm in arm, we each carried a statue to the Hotel Monchsburg. Without speaking, we walked right past my room and went into Sigmund's. He barely let me set the statue down before pulling me toward the big, soft bed.

Now, late at night, I can watch him sleep. I fancy to breathe every breath with him. Can one die from happiness?

## July 18, 1897

Our love has blossomed like the flowers outside our windows. We have been three days in this wonderland and life is glorious. Every touch of our bodies is magic, and we have discarded all pretense of modesty. When he is fully satisfied by our lovemaking, Sigmund sets to work at his desk with a fury.

"Minna, the interpretation of dreams becomes clearer and clearer," he says with enthusiasm. Then, after several hours, seized by sensual feelings again, he finds me and we make love like two free animals in the woods.

I am wearing nothing but a silk dressing gown, and Sigmund frequently pauses at his work to open the gown and caress my body. He kisses me and breathes in my scent before turning back to his work.

I yield to his desires and our passion is uncontrollable, as if it will swallow us both, as if we cease to be two people and become one.

"Minna," Sigmund said after one of our ecstasies, "my world is opening. With you, I suddenly see the whole range of sexuality and what it means. Before this, my thoughts had focused on the physical, but I see beyond it to a power of the mind." He trailed off, deep in thought for a moment. "A primal energy, beyond any I have known," he finished with amazement.

We have left the room only to eat and take brief walks. The fragrances have never been so sweet, so pungent, and the food — it is as if I have never truly tasted before. Last night, I had *Tauben mit Pilzen* and the squab was elegant; the mushrooms contained all the goodness of the earth. The *Nusstorte* was indescribably delicious and the background strain of

145

rum made me think of food as a symphony. Every one of my senses is enlivened.

## July 19, 1897

I love him with all my heart and soul. The days are clear outside and there is a sun deep within us as well. Everything is lush. He gives me daisies and roses and they radiate more beauty than I ever knew this earth contained. I realized with a start that there is so much beauty we miss every day in our ordinary lives.

God forgive me for the love of a man I should not love. And yet, I feel that without this man, I would cease to be.

## July 21, 1897

Sigi and I hiked to the Heilbronn arm in arm this morning. At midday, he told me of a surprise. "In ancient times, men thought of this as the death and rebirth of the world, as a sign from God."

"Whatever do you mean, Sigi?" I asked.

"Look up, Minna. It is beginning."

I looked at the sun and saw it slowly covered by a black circle until it was almost gone. Only a slight glow was left around its edges. "A sign from God," I gasped, clutching his arm more firmly.

Sigmund laughed. "It is the solar eclipse, Minna. Haven't you read about it in the newspaper?"

"Oh Sigi, it is a sign, don't you see? A sign that nothing is permanent, that we should grasp and hold tight to what we have in the present because it can all disappear!" I buried my face against his rough woolen vest, overcome by fear and emotion.

Sigmund, surprised by my sudden outburst, soothed me as the sun returned to its full fury. We did not discuss the episode later, but I know that we both saw clearly that this precious time together would soon end.

## July 29, 1897

Our final day together. How absurd because we will live in the same house and share the same dinner table. But this is our last day together. For dinner, Sigmund took me to a very expensive restaurant — far too expensive, I said, but he shushed me. I dressed in my very best and wore the garnet ear bobs that Mama gave me shortly after Papa died. Her mother had passed them down to her.

We had a lovely red wine with our meal that made me slightly tipsy. Sigmund looked across the table with adoration while I prattled on and on about this and that. Even in my intoxicated state, however, I was careful not to mention tomorrow.

Later, as we made love, it was different. We were together, not in a frenzy of passion but slowly, almost as if trying to imprint this time permanently upon our memories.

I know it must end, but with all my heart, I wish we could run away together, to a different land and a different time. The destination matters not. Only that we are together.

## August 1, 1897

After our splendid vacation, I was afraid to face Martha again. It was the hardest act of my life, fearing that she would read my mind and discover the secrets of my heart. I felt like my love for Sigmund must be emblazoned across my being. Yet I had to face her; we needed to return to the family at Bad Aussee. A carriage delivered us from the train station, and I trembled as we approached the cottage. Sigmund kissed me softly on the forehead and then moved to the seat opposite me. There was sadness in his eyes. The sun was setting in the west, leaving an orange glow to light our way back.

Martha bustled out as I alighted from the carriage. "How blissful you look, Minna. Hiking in the mountains is good for your constitution." She gave me a warm embrace and pecked a kiss on my cheek. Holding my hand, she said, "Where is my Sigi?"

"There he is," I said, "getting the baggage out of the carriage." I pointed to the far side of the vehicle. I wondered how Martha could express such warmth – such kindness – to me, the lover of her husband. Can't she see?

"Sigi, *mein liebtchen*, come to me," she called fervently to her husband. He set the bags down on the ground and embraced her. "Are you well? Ah yes, good. The children are fine. Sophie was stung by a wasp yesterday, but such minor calamities are expected. I'm so glad to have you home." She herded Sigi, who was laden with the baggage, inside to the cottage. I took one last glance at the darkening horizon, drawing strength from its beauty. "Remember," I told myself, "to be near to Sigmund is worth everything."

Inside, Martha was surveying Sigmund's hiking outfit – his jaunty green Tirol hat, gray Norfolk jacket, leather knickers, gray wool socks, and his favorite forest boots. "You look wonderful, mein Sigi, so much more relaxed than the black-suited Viennese doctor I usually see. Even you have said that for the bow to be strong it must remain unstrung for a time."

"It was a very refreshing and lovely hike, wasn't it, Minna?" Sigmund said, shifting uncomfortably. It appeared to me that he avoided Martha's eyes, but she didn't seem to notice.

The children discovered our arrival and attacked, hugging and demanding to be told every detail of our travels. Sigmund began by describing the huge castle, and they listened with wide eyes, enraptured by the tale he was weaving.

"Please wash for dinner," Marty called out over the noise. "I have a treat – we've been working on it all day."

"Perhaps I could see Anna for a few moments before getting ready?" I asked.

"Of course, Minna," Martha said graciously. "Anna has been missing you. Josephine is here, of course, but still Anna asks every day for her Tante Minna."

I found her in the nursery building with blocks, and as she heard my footsteps, she looked up. "Tante Minna! Tante Minna!" she cried excitedly over and over again. She ran to me, knocking over her tower of blocks, and jumped into my arms. Clinging, she nuzzled at my neck and showered me with kisses. I had missed her so.

We remained for quite some time, just Anna and me, rocking

together in silence. I stroked her soft skin and hair until she fell asleep and then joined the others for dinner.

## October 4, 1897

### Vienna

The remaining summer days passed quickly, and I have not confided in you, my dearest friend, for weeks. I carry my memories close to my heart every waking moment and have spent many nights dreaming of my love.

We returned to Vienna last night. The journey always seems longer returning from a vacation than it does going. As usual, the children were all tired and quite ill-tempered by the time we arrived home. Thank heavens for Josephine.

The air here feels heavy and dirty. I'm afraid I've become accustomed to the clean mountain air and the bright sunshine. I have an urge to throw open all the windows and pull back the heavy velvet draperies. Wouldn't Marty be horrified!

I've spent many hours studying Sigmund's paper, *Sexuality and the Etiology of the Neuroses.* I found an error and wanted to bring it to his attention but did not want to create a rift in our relationship. We have settled into an easy, comfortable status, somehow being able to set aside our passions now that we have had a chance to express them so fully. I must admit, though, that he can make my breath quicken and my blood course just by touching me.

"Sigmund," I said, after checking to see if he was with a patient, "in your article *Sexuality and the . . .*"

He interrupted me. "Yes, Minna. What of it?" He was preoccupied with a new project.

"Well, I have been reading it," I said hesitantly, "and I see that you have not yet changed the sentence discussing an early childhood sexual experience as the root of all hysteria."

"I've gone over that paper several times and am sure that it is not there. Show me what you are talking about." He spoke rather gruffly.

I pointed to the passage I had marked and he frowned. "You are right. I suppose part of me doesn't want to give up that theory."

"And," Sigmund looked up, not quite so preoccupied now, as I continued with more confidence, "another aspect, Sigi, is that you write that it is generally said that a physician has no right to intrude upon his patients' privacy in sexual matters or to wound their modesty, but you don't go on to explain your disagreement in detail. With an enemy like Krafft-Ebing, your writing must leave no doubt as to the professional necessity of such questioning."

"Yes, that is a good point," Sigi agreed. "What did you think about my treatment of the lack of sexual gratification and the symptoms?"

"Well," I began, sitting down in the armchair across from his desk, "I wondered why you did not mention addictions, such as those we had discussed. I recall you saying that the addict tries to find a substitute for missing sexual gratification and that the treatment of such cravings will be ineffective until the patient has a satisfying sexual life."

Sigmund nodded enthusiastically. "Another excellent point, Minna."

I felt embarrassed by his praise. "Thank you, Sigi," I said demurely.

He was now sitting bolt upright in his chair. Apparently I had gotten his full attention. "Minna, at this rate, you will soon be asking for the title of coauthor — and then we would be in danger of getting into a spat like the one between Josef Breuer and myself. Before long, we would not be speaking to one another."

"That could never happen, Sigi," I laughed coquettishly. "I have no desire to take over your work. I was thinking about your translation of John Stuart Mill and how the essays on social problems — labor, the enfranchisement of women, and socialism — were partly the work of his wife."

"Yes," Sigmund agreed, "but despite his views on the emancipation of women, he did not emancipate her enough to include her name." This was added sarcastically.

"But I don't want my name on it, Sigmund," I said quickly. "I am not like Lou-Kind after all, and I don't have university and medical degrees. Who would listen if my name were on it?" I suddenly leaned across the desk and kissed him. "The world will recognize you, and *you* will recognize me."

"Your forwardness is becoming," Sigi said, returning my kiss with one of his own.

He is pleased when I am bold, and pleasing him pleases me. It is amazing how simple things have become.

## October 10, 1897

Marty and I took a long walk around the Ringstrasse, chatting about this and that. The big news recently was about the duel between Count Badeni, the prime minister, and Dr. Wolff of the Parliament. It seems that Wolff called Badeni a Polish pig and Badeni countered by implying that Wolff's parentage was in doubt. The German Nationalist leader took this as the most extreme insult possible. Wolff did not instigate the duel because he feared the five-year jail penalty, but Badeni, being immune, challenged him to a duel. Some say that Badeni wouldn't have done it without Franz Josef's backing, but the emperor is now in Hungary for a meeting with Russia's Emperor William and refused comment. Rumor has it that old Franz Josef was wearing the uniform of a Prussian field marshal and the ribbon of the Order of the Black Eagle. Then, once business was finished, he tried to send an urgent message to "the Schratt" to join him because he was lonely. Marty and I giggled over this foolishness like schoolgirls. We hadn't felt this close for years.

"Minna. Look there," Martha said as we passed Maria Theresien-strasse. "The first place Sigi and I lived together was there at Number 8. It is the Suhnhaus, the house of atonement, named because it is built on the very spot of the old Ring theatre that burned down in 1881. It was such an elegant place, but we were very young and could hardly afford the sixteen hundred gulden each month."

"You rarely talk about those times, Martha."

"I suppose I don't. Mathilde was highly honored there as the first baby born in the Suhnhaus—a new life from the old. The emperor himself sent an imperial porcelain vase and a signed certificate."

"What happened to it?"

"We gave it to Amalie," Martha said, laughing. "You know, she claims that her birthday, August 18, is the same as the emperor's, but that is only because she wanted it that way and made it up since she couldn't use the Jewish calendar. She loves royalty and the vase is one of her prize treasures now. Material things mattered little to us then. As long as we had enough for the basic necessities, we were very happy."

"Why don't you talk about it? Were there problems?" I asked curiously.

"The biggest problem scarcely seems like a problem now, but I was so frightened with the first baby, and then I was with child again so soon afterward with hardly any time to get used to having children." Martha's voice was soft. "The labor was hard for me, and having children meant more mouths to feed. Sigmund wanted the best for us and was hard to satisfy. Once he gave me a snake bracelet, a kind of status symbol for university doctors. It was beautiful and I loved it, but he made me put it away because it was silver and he was ashamed that he didn't have the money for gold."

I could well imagine Sigmund requesting such a thing.

"You see," Martha went on, "a good address seemed very important to develop a thriving practice, and such luminaries lived near here. The composer Anton Bruckner lived across the street on Hessgasse. The Kursalon was nearby, and we could walk there and see young people doing whirling waltzes — so much faster than they dance now. The strains of Strauss's waltzes could be heard from our window if the wind was right."

"Did you go out much?" I asked, wanting to know more about this time in their lives.

"Occasionally to the opera. We were mostly content to stay home. Sometimes I could bring Sigi out to see *Don Giovanni*, but I had a hard time dragging him to concerts. He never wanted to go to any of the grand balls. He claimed he didn't like the music and that the dancing made him ill." Martha laughed — a very young, lighthearted laugh that I hadn't heard in years. "He was always so serious then — in some ways he is younger now."

As we passed the opera house, Martha looked at the newly completed massive building with its ornate arches and huge doors. She stopped and we peered inside.

"You know, Minna, Vienna is a place of suicides. The architect

152

of this opera house killed himself after it was built. He felt that no one appreciated his ingenious design. Crown Prince Rudolf killed himself when we lived in the Suhnhaus. We used to see his fiacre passing by with the driver Bratfisch.

"I feel better now, but after Anna's birth, I went into such a depression that I didn't know if I could survive." Martha's tone had changed. "There were times when I thought the world would be a better place without me."

"Martha," I said, hugging her. "We were all with you during that time. I wouldn't have let you go."

She walked on in silence for several steps. "I never really thought about it seriously before. It was just one day, when the Fohn wind was blowing in from the mountains, I got an eerie, unsettled feeling and began to think of ways to end my life. I might have done it if it wasn't for Sigi and you. Just knowing you were there, and that you were helping him, gave me comfort, Minna."

My guilt welled up once again. I ached to know just how much she was aware of my relationship with Sigi. Her sincere words had touched my heart, and I felt a great rush of love for my older sister. Perhaps Sigmund was not the only one benefiting from my being with the family. This thought helped to ease the tightness in my chest.

"The most important thing," Martha said as we reached the door of our apartment, "is that we are family and will always be together to take care of one another."

I am so blessed.

## November 12, 1897

Oliver has lost two teeth now, one on the fifth of November and one just this afternoon. The other children are jealous and are wiggling away at their teeth.

It is hard to believe how quickly they are growing. They have all changed so since I joined the family just two years ago.

Annerl is no longer a baby but is an independent person on her own. I guess we must all learn and grow.

## December 2, 1897

Ida Fleiss paid us a visit last night. Although she could only stay for one night, it was very pleasant and Martha enjoyed the company.

Sigmund would love to meet with Wilhelm and asked her numerous questions about his health, his work, and his travel plans. I do hope they can meet up before too long. It is so important to Sigi's work.

## December 15, 1897

My wish has come true. Sigi is traveling to Breslau to meet with Wilhelm. Although he will be gone for most of Hanukkah, I am so pleased. I do hope it will be a productive and satisfying congress. I shall miss him dreadfully.

# 1898

## January 1, 1898

For months now, I have been helping Sigmund write his book about dreams. We are deeply involved in the manuscript. When we finish work each night, we often make love, and our work together grows still more beautiful.

Dreams have become another world for me. Sometimes I am anxious to sleep to have more time to dream. I can now understand the ancient Greeks and Orientals who would not undertake a military campaign without a dream interpreter, much as we use scouts or spies.

My dreams always begin from some stimulus — a happening during the day, a discussion with a shopkeeper, an event with the children — but then the elaborations lead me deeper into myself. Sigmund says, "The person in analysis knows the answers to his own problems. Psycho-analysis is a way I can help him find them" — and this is true with myself. *I know* — even when I think I don't know. The associations lead me to my truth, except when I can go no further because some cluster of memories is too disagreeable to invoke. "A complex," Sigi calls it. I need him to help me in such cases, and he listens, helping me unleash my "complexes" and understand them.

It is a sign of the closeness of our relationship that he can help me to interpret my dreams. This means that I have no secrets from him — not even those of my sleeping state. I love him with all my being and give freely of all myself.

Already Sigi is beginning plans for a book to explore all the forms of sexuality. His thoughts seem to be maturing, more balanced now, and he can see issues in polarities, with male and female forces.

"Life is worth living again!" Sigi rejoiced to me last night after an entire evening spent going over just twenty pages of the dream book. "My desire for revenge on Krafft-Ebing is fading compared to the greatness of this task — the understanding of the psychic life in which men spend one-third of their time on earth."

"And women," I reminded him softly.

"And women. Yes, dear Minna, and women," he chuckled naughtily. "Who would think that I could forget about women!"

## March 17, 1898

Sigmund is so excited lately. Tonight, he sat down at the dinner table and immediately began talking about his work. "The dream is a wish fulfillment. Desire is at the root of every dream," he announced over the *huhnersuppe*.

Martha was annoyed. "Perhaps at the family dinner table it is best not to discuss matters of psychoanalysis. You and Minna can speak of it together, later."

Sigmund, slightly taken aback, looked at me with raised eyebrows. At that moment, we were connected on all levels as comrades, lovers, friends. The feeling was very powerful and left me with a deep sense of contentment.

## August 1, 1898

I met Sigmund in Munich, where he had just finished a congress with Wilhelm.

"He is still a bit put out, Minna, over my Easter trip with Alexander, but I assured him of the depth of our friendship. His distance disturbs me."

"And his comments about the dream book?" I asked, knowing that Sigi had been anxiously awaiting Wilhelm's insights.

"We didn't talk much about it," Sigi said with some disappointment. "We visited sights, enjoyed restaurants, and talked about Conrad Ferdinand Meyer's books." He was silent for a moment. "But we did discuss the inscription for the dream book."

"Did he like 'wavering phantoms, you approach again . . .' your idea from Faust?" I asked.

"No, he suggested a quotation from *Paradise Lost*."

"And?" I asked. "What about *The Aeneid*—the part we read to each other?"

"That's my choice, Minna. I decided to go to Virgil. In Juno's words, *Flectere si nequeo superos, Acheronta movebo.* If I cannot change Heaven, I shall stir up Hell. And this book shall do that, I promise."

## August 2, 1898

As the horse-drawn wagon creaked and almost slid into a ravine going across the Stelvio Pass from Trafoi, Sigmund leaned out to ask the driver, "How much farther?" The wind at the top felt cold as we passed the areas of perennial snow on our way to Bormio.

"About halfway," the driver shouted back in Italian, pointing to an old stone shelter used by tired or snowed-in hikers and travelers.

"With this much snow they might even close the pass in September instead of at the end of October," Sigmund mused as we sat back in the cab. The driver skillfully negotiated a steep serpentine and we began our descent.

"Imagine Hannibal crossing such passes in winter. No wonder his was a surprise attack."

Sigmund nodded his assent but his mind was elsewhere. "Minna, to publish the dream book means that I must expose my innermost life to a prying public. Can I risk it?"

"Do you have any choice?" I answered. "Can you create a book using only the dreams of your patients or those told to you by other doctors?"

He thought for a moment, his eyes roaming the sunlit jagged top of the mountain ranges, watching the snow blowing off the peaks in fine flurries. "I cannot afford not to publish the book," he said solemnly. "I cannot be that selfish. I can't keep for myself the most beautiful discovery I have ever made and perhaps the only one that will survive me."

"I had a dream last night, Sigi," I said, nestling close to him in the small cab and pulling our plaid woolen blanket about us. "I dreamed that we were together on a hill or mountainside. We were lying in the sunshine, surrounded by yellow flowers and high yellow wheat. The sensation was incredibly warm and comforting. We were filled with love and joy, but then it began getting cold and we had to leave. It grew darker as we found a path leading uphill. Finally, we came through a narrow and dark tunnel, which I first thought wouldn't end, but we emerged into a place filled with bright light and the warm feeling returned. Like a feeling of a spirit entering me."

"And your associations, Minna?" he encouraged.

"The associations of the warm place all had to do with safety, love, security, being cared for, and home, the darkness and cold were distress, fear, guilt, struggle."

"So, we went together through the dark and narrow tunnel and emerged into bright light," Sigmund mused.

I thought for a moment. "It sounds like the story of Orpheus, who descended into the underworld to bring back his love, Eurydice, who had died from an asp bite. He gains permission because of the purity of his love for her. As he ascends from the underworld, he is instructed that she will follow, but he must not look at her until they are in the light. They pass through the entire tunnel, but then as he enters the sun-drenched upper world, he turns to see her, but she, still in the shadows, must return to the underworld and death again."

"I am like that Orpheus with you, Minna, but from the descent I have returned with you and the greatest treasure – my work – to unlock the secrets of dreams. Soon, like Orpheus with his lyre, I will play my song to the world," Sigi told me softly. Together we listened to the rhythmic sound of the wagon wheels. It felt timeless in this faraway place.

"Is our love pure, Sigi?" I asked, thinking about the story. He answered me with a kiss.

## August 3, 1898

We finally arrived in Bormio and have taken a sunny little room at a small inn. Love and dreams again.

## August 4, 1898

Today we set out to Tirano. From there, we shall hike up the valley to the village of Le Prese, on the shore of Lake Poschiavo.

I was looking at a map spread out on the bed, planning our route, while Sigmund sat at a small desk writing. "Like a dream, Minna. The material is coming like a dream."

We are set apart from the world. I saw a newspaper in Bormio, but events of the world seem far away and unimportant. The big news headline was the tsar's manifesto. I brought the newspaper to Sigi.

"The peace conference," he said, looking up. "I diagnosed the young tsar some years ago as suffering from obsessional ideas and, fortunately for us, fear of blood. His words about avoiding militancy and the unnecessary economic burden of war are so revolutionary that were he not the tsar he would be sent to Siberia — and have all his remarks censored." Sigi laughed freely now without the tightness I have often heard in his voice in Vienna.

"At least it is a call for peace," I remarked.

"Like asking a seething unconscious to settle down," Sigi responded. "Peace cannot come so easily."

"You and I have found peace," I said, encircling him with my arms.

Sigmund firmly rolled the newspaper and put it in the wicker wastebasket. "Let us put away all papers — whether good news or bad. They are an emotional burden taking us away from our dreams of each other."

## August 5, 1898

Lake Poschiavo — deep blue, ringed by snowcapped mountains, with fresh red berries on the sloping banks and hills. La Prese, an idyllic village with just-picked violet grapes and oranges abounding, happy people, vines growing on the hills in orderly rows, and everywhere little old ladies with kerchiefs pulling overflowing high-sided wagons.

"I feel like a peasant lady carrying my dream book and thoughts with us — like a wagon of fruit," Sigmund said, laughing. "Now I see how dreams are made, how the idea starts from an event in life and becomes aligned with a deep wish. The dream we finally have has gone through all that 'dream work.' Here, I have written all my ideas out for you, Minna." He gave me a sheaf of papers covered with his sloping scrawl containing ideas, metaphors, fragments of dreams. On the front was written "To Minna."

I began to read aloud. "What we recollect as the dream after we have awakened is not the true dream process but is a facade behind which the process lies concealed. What we see is manifest — what lies behind are 'latent dream thoughts.' The way the manifest comes from the latent I call

162

the dream work – all the distortions, condensations, and symbols come from the secondary elaboration. At the heart of the dream is a wish."

## August 6, 1898

We took a carriage across the Bernina Pass to the Engadine. Perhaps there is no place in the world more powerful than the top of that pass – wild isolation, a windy place of incomparable beauty. The carriage swayed to and fro, creaking in the wind coming from the Italian Alps on one side, from the Swiss Alps on the other.

"I live as if on another planet so far from the other world," I said aloud. It is just he and I now, together, concentrating our energies, focusing them, helping each other, loving each other. We have harnessed the power of the unconscious. I have never known such happiness.

"Remember this feeling we have, Minna. Write down your sensations and return to them. This is peace. If the world knew of this, there would be no wars."

Later, after we stopped for the night at the Hotel Firino in Potresina, Sigmund sprawled back in his chair. He had that slightly rumpled look that I had begun to prize. It meant that finally his mind was not on his work but on life. "We will be rich, Minna," he announced. "When this book is published, patients will flock to my door. Everybody who has ever had a dream will want to use my technique to analyze it properly."

"Will it really mean all that?" I asked hesitantly, kneeling on the floor at his feet.

"All that and more. A new house in Grinnzing, satin and lace, gold and diamonds, new clothes for the family. Amalie will dress like the royalty she is, and my reputation will spread over Europe and all the continents. This work is inspired, Minna. It is an opening, a window granted to me only once in my lifetime. Then softly, he quoted Shakespeare. " 'There is a tide in the affairs of men, which, taken at the flood, leads on to fortune.' I feel as close to doing God's work as an enthusiastic new minister," he chuckled.

Caught up in Sigi's excitement, I saw in my mind our new home with rooms for all the children, the family together, warm and happy, away from the dreary old city, never having to fret about money. We would be so happy in our love. We would spend our time reading, writing, loving, discovering, exploring. We could travel whenever we desired.

"To Rome," I said aloud. "We will go to Rome."

I had a vision of Sigi holding his dream book, his eyes bright, lecturing on a podium to crowds of avid listeners who had come from all over the world to hear his words — a sea of uplifted faces.

He rose and lifted me from the floor. We pressed ourselves together into a tight embrace, and joy filled me, along with peace — a calm, tranquil peace — beyond any I had ever known before, and as his arms encircled me, our spirits joined and I was cleaved unto him.

# Epilogue

A cough startled me back to the present, and I looked up, half expecting to see Sigmund Freud. It was only Walter Amend, the shopkeeper, telling me he was closing. The sun had long since set, and it was dark outside – time for his dinner.

I asked him what the price would be for the two books that I cradled in my lap – not being able to bear the thought of leaving them behind. He waved me off, saying that there was nothing worth paying for in this room full of junk. Although I tried to tell him the value of the books, he was agitated and in a hurry to close the shop. He rushed me out through the front door, snapping the lock behind me.

While shrugging my shoulders to relieve a cramp in my neck, I took a deep breath of the cool evening air and wondered how long I had perched in that dusty little room. In a daze, I wandered down the Floriangasse, oblivious to the world around me.

Upon reaching my pension, I entered the house quietly, not yet willing to be parted from Minna and the images of her world. The heavy front door creaked open on its old hinges, and I closed it furtively. As I mounted the worn steps that led to my room, the aged wood moaned with my weight, and my landlady called out from the parlor that there was some dinner left. I pretended not to hear and escaped to my room.

Safely inside, I slung my backpack onto a nail in the wall, clicked on the lamp beside my favorite overstuffed chair, and sank comfortably into the cushions. I gently fingered the delicate, fraying pages of the brown velvet-covered book, frustrated that there was not more to read. What had happened to Minna? What was her life like in the years after her narrative abruptly ended?

A soft knock brought me out of my musings, and I reluctantly opened the door.

There, in the harsh light of the hallway, stood someone I had never again expected to see. For a moment, all sense of reality disappeared, and I wondered if this could be a dream.

"Surprise!" said the man I loved. "I've left her, my dear. I traveled all night to be with you. You are all that I could ever want." He reached out to me, and I instinctively moved across the threshold into his arms.

Past and present became one. I finally understood what was important in this lifetime. I was now complete.

# Afterword

It was eight years before the six hundred copies of *The Interpretation of Dreams* were sold. There were years of struggle, but Minna's strength and her faith in Sigmund's work remained as unwavering as her love.

In 1902, the Wednesday Night Psychological Association (which later evolved into the International Psychoanalytic Association) was formed. The original group of five physician-members, who met to discuss various aspects of psychoanalysis, had been organized by Wilhelm Stekel, who was joined shortly thereafter by Dr. Alfred Adler, an early student of Freud's who at that time was much impressed by *The Interpretation of Dreams*. The meetings were held at Freud's home, where it was natural for Minna to be in attendance, providing such creature comforts as cigars, coffee, and other refreshments. When the guests had left, she and Sigmund would continue the discussion late into the night. In this way, she helped him clarify his ideas for his later works – *Psychopathology of Everyday Life*, *Wit and the Relation to the Unconscious*, and his *Three Essays on the Theory of Sexuality*.

Baron Richard von Krafft-Ebing died suddenly at the age of sixty-two, and shortly thereafter, Freud was offered and immediately accepted the appointment of Professor Extraordinarius. By that time, however, this honor had lost much of its meaning.

The children grew up and fared well – except for Sophie, "the Sunday child," who left two children when she died, at the age of twenty-seven, in an influenza epidemic. The entire family grieved deeply over this loss.

In 1938, the family, including Minna, moved to London from Vienna to escape the Nazi Anschluss. Amalie had died six years before and was spared the horror of Nazi occupation.

U.S. President Franklin D. Roosevelt, aided by the recommendation of the Italian Fascist Premier Benito Mussolini, intervened on behalf of the Freud family and convinced the Nazi regime to provide safe passage to the family in exchange for a large ransom provided by Princess Maria

Bonaparte, a wealthy French student of psychoanalysis.

In London, Paula Fichtl, the housekeeper, arranged Freud's study almost exactly as it had been in Vienna – under Minna's direction.

Minna Bernays never married. She remained with the Freud family until Sigmund's death on September 23, 1939, at the age of eighty-three. He had been in great pain and required numerous operations due to cancer of the jaw. Minna nursed him faithfully until the end. By that time, her vision was impaired and she was also suffering from recurrent pulmonary disease.

Minna's physical condition rapidly deteriorated after Sigmund's death, and she died a little more than one year after he did. Martha, who had completely regained her health, remained alive until 1950.

Little Anna, the child closest to Sigmund and Minna, never married. She devoted herself to preserving her father's legacy and took over a great deal of work in the psychoanalytic association. Her great work, particularly with children, is recognized as a unique contribution in its own right. As she grew, Anna competed with Minna for her father's attention. Their relationship became strained. Anna Freud died in 1982.

Ironically, Anna became custodian of Freud's letters, papers, and photographs. As the years have passed, Minna's involvement with the Freud family was minimized to conceal the relationship. Dates and documents show marked discrepancies when discussing "Tante Minna." At the time of this writing, many photographs and letters still have not been released to the public.

# BIBLIOGRAPHY

Anziew, Didier. *Freud's Self-Analysis*. London: Hogarth Press and the Institute of Psycho-Analysis, 1986.

Assagioli, Roberto, M.D. *The Act of Will*. New York: Penguin Books, 1973.

Bailey, Percival. *Sigmund the Unserene*. Springfield, NJ: Charles C. Thomas, 1965.

Balogh, Penelope. *Freud - A Biographical Introduction*. New York: Charles Scribners Sons, 1971.

Bernays, Anna Freud. "My Brother, Sigmund Freud." *The American Mercury* 51:335-42.

Bernays, Anne. *Professor Romeo*. London: Weidenfeld & Nicolson, 1989.

Binion, Rudolph. *Frau Lou*. Princeton, NJ: Princeton University Press, 1968.

Bond, Jules J. *The Viennese Cuisine I Love*. Leon Amiel, Publisher, 1977.

Bottome, Phyllis. *Alfred Adler*. New York: The Vanguard Press, 1957.

Brenner, Charles. *An Elementary Textbook of Psychoanalysis*. New York: Doubleday & Co., Inc., 1957.

Brome, Vincent. *Freud and His Early Circle*. New York: William Morrow & Co. Inc., 1967.

Byck, Robert, M.D., ed. *Cocaine Papers by Sigmund Freud*. New York: New American Library, 1974.

Campbell, Joseph, ed. *The Portable Jung*. New York: Viking Press, 1971.

Cartocci, Sergio. *Rome As It Was*. Rome: Art Publishers, 1974.

Charcot, J. M. *Lectures on the Diseases of the Nervous System*. New York: Hafner Publishing Co., 1962.

Costigan, Giovanni. *Sigmund Freud*. New York: Macmillan Co. 1965.

Delecluze, Etienne-Jean. *Two Lovers in Rome*. Garden City, NY: Doubleday & Co., Inc., 1958.

Dunaway, Philip & Evans, Mel, eds. *A Treasury of the World's Great Diaries*. Garden City, NY: Doubleday and Co. Inc., 1957.

Edwards, Tudor. *The Blue Danube*. London: Robert Hale, 1973.

Ellenberger, Henri R. *The Discovery of the Unconscious*. New York: Basic Books, Inc., 1970.

Elon, Amos. *Herzl*. New York: Holt, Rinehart &Winston, 1975.

Engelman, Edmund. *Bergasse 19 :Sigmund Freud's Home and Offices, Vienna, 1938*. New York: Basic Books, Inc., 1976.

Evans-Wentz, W. Y., ed. *The Tibetan Book of the Dead*. New York: Oxford University, 1960.

Fontane, Theodor. *Effi Briest*. New York: Penguin Books, 1967.

Freud, Ernst, Freud, Lucie, & Grubrich-Simitis, Ilse. *Sigmund Freud*. New York and London: Basic Books, Inc. 1976.

Freud, Ernst L., ed. *The Letters of Sigmund Freud*. New York: Basic Books, Inc., 1960

____. *The Letters of Sigmund Freud and Arnold Zweig*. New York: Harcourt Brace Jovanovich, Inc., 1970.

Freud, Martin. *Glory Reflected*. London: Angus & Robertson, 1952.

____. *Sigmund Freud: Man and Father*. New York: Vanguard Press. 1955.

Freud, Sigmund. *A General Introduction to Psychoanalysis*. Translated by Joan Riviere. New York: Liveright Publishing Co., 1935.

____. *A General Introduction to Psychoanalysis*. New York: Pocket Books, 1972.

____. *An Outline of Psychoanalysis*. New York: W. W. Norton & Co., Inc., 1949.

____. *Beyond the Pleasure Principle*. New York: W. W. Norton & Co., Inc., 1961.

____. *Character and Culture*. New York: Collier Books, 1963.

____. *Civilization and Its Discontents*. Translated by Joan Riviere. London: Hogarth Press, 1946.

____. *Early Psychoanalytic Writings*. New York: Collier Books, 1963.

____. *Freud's Principles of Psychoanalysis*. Edited by A.A. Brill. Garden City, NY: Garden City Books, 1953.

____. *Jokes and Their Relation to the Unconscious*. New York: W. W. Norton & Co., Inc., 1960.

____. *Leonardo DaVinci*. New York: Vintage Books, 1947.

____. *Moses and Monotheism*. New York: Alfred A. Knopf, 1939.

____. *On the History of the Psychoanalytic Movement*. New York: W. W. Norton & Co., Inc., 1966.

____. *Sexuality and the Psychology of Love*. New York: Collier Books, 1974.

____. *The Basic Writings of Sigmund Freud*. Edited by A. A. Brill. New York: Modern Library, 1938.

____. *The Ego and the Id*. New York: W. W. Norton & Co., Inc., 1960.

____. *The Ego and the Id*. Translated by Joan Riviere. Edited by James Strachey. New York: W.W. Norton & Co., Inc., 1962.

____. *The Interpretation of Dreams*. Translated by A.A. Brill. London: Allen & Unwin, 1927.

____. *The Interpretation of Dreams*. New York: Avon Books, 1965.

____. *The Origin and Development of Psychoanalysis*. Chicago: Henry Regnery Co. , 1955.

____. *The Origins of Psychoanalysis - Letters to Wilhelm Fliess*. New York: Basic Books, Inc. 1954.

____. *Psychopathology of Everyday Life*. New York: W. W. Norton & Co., Inc., 1965.

____. *The Sexual Enlightenment of Children*. New York: Collier Books, 1963.

____. *Three Contributions to the Theory of Sex*. New York: E. P. Dutton & Co., Inc., 1962.

____. *Three Essays on the Theory of Sexuality*. New York: Basic Books, Inc., 1962.

____. *Totem and Taboo*. New York: Vintage Books, 1918.

Freud, Sigmund & Breuer, Josef. *Studies in Hysteria*. New York: Avon, 1966.

Fromm, Erich. *Sigmund Freud's Mission*. New York: Grove Press, Inc., 1959.

Gainham, Sarah. *Night Falls on the City*. New York: Holt, Rinehart & Winston, 1967.

Gay, Peter. *Freud, Jews and Other Germans*. New York: Oxford University Press, 1978.

Goethe, Johann Wolfgang. *Faust - Part One*. New York: Penguin Books, 1949.

Grant, Michael. *History of Rome*. New York: Charles Scribners & Sons, 1978.

Gunther, John. *The Lost City*. New York: Harper & Row, 1964.

Hamilton, Edith. *Mythology*. New York: New American Library, 1940.

Harner, Michael J., ed. *Hallucinogens and Shamanism*. New York: Oxford University Press, 1973.

___. *The Way of the Shaman*. New York: Harper & Row, 1980.

Hellerstein, Edna, et al., eds. *Victorian Women*. Stanford, CA: Stanford University Press, 1981.

Hendricks, Rhoda A. *Classical Gods and Heroes: Myths as Told by the Ancient Authors*. New York: William Morrow & Co., 1974.

Higgins, Mary, et al., eds. *Reich Speaks of Freud*. New York: Noonday Press, 1967.

Hirschfeld, Ludwig. *The Vienna That's Not in the Baedeker*. Edited by T. W. MacCallum. Verlag Munchen: R. Piper & Co., 1929.

Horney, Karen. *The Adolescent Diaries of Karen Horney*. New York: Basic Books, Inc. 1980.

Huson, Paul. *Mastering Witchcraft*. New York: G. P. Putnam's Sons, 1980.

Janik, Allan & Toulmin, Stephen, eds. *Wittgenstein's Vienna*. New York: Simon & Schuster, 1973.

Johns, June. *King of the Witches*. New York: Coward-McCann, 1969.

Jones, Ernest, ed. *The International Psychoanalytical Library*. London: Hogarth Press, 1946.

___. M.D. *The Life and Work of Sigmund Freud, Vol. 1*. New York: Basic Books, Inc., 1953.

___. *The Life and Work of Sigmund Freud*. Edited by Lionel Trilling and Steven Marcus. New York: Basic Books, Inc., 1961.

Jung, C. G. *Memories, Dreams, Reflections*. New York: Vintage Books, 1965.

Lawrence, D. H. *The Plumed Serpent*. New York: Vintage Books, 1959.

Learsi, Rufus. *Fulfillment: The Epic Story of Zionism*. New York: World Publishing Co. 1951.

Leavy, Stanley A. *The Freud Journal of Lou Andreas-Salome*. New York: Basic Books, Inc., 1964.

Lesky, R. *The Vienna Medical School of the Nineteenth Century*. Baltimore, MD: Johns Hopkins University Press, 1976.

Lindner, Robert, ed. & Staff, Clement, assoc. ed. *Explorations in Psychoanalysis*. New York: Julian Press, Inc., 1953.

Mannoni, O. *Freud*. New York: Pantheon Books, 1971.

Marmor, Judd, ed. *Modern Psychoanalysis: New Directions and Perspectives*. New York: Basic Books, Inc., 1968.

Masters, R. E. L. *Eros and Evil*. New York: Julian Press, Inc., 1962.

Meng, Heinrich & Freud, Ernst. *Psychoanalysis and Faith: The Letters of Sigmund Freud and Oskar Pfeister*. Translated by Eric Mosbacher. New York: Basic Books, Inc. 1963.

Menninger, Karl A. *Man Against Himself*. New York: Harcourt, Brace and Company, 1938.

Moffat, Mary Jane & Painter, Charlotte, eds. *Revelations - Diaries of Women*. New York: Vintage Books, 1974.

Mortimer, W. Golden, M.D. *History of Coca*. San Francisco: And/Or Press, 1974.

Morton, Frederic. *A Nervous Splendor*. New York: Penguin Books, 1979.

Neider, Charles, ed. *The Complete Essays of Mark Twain*. Garden City, NY: Doubleday & Co., Inc., 1963.

Nelson, Benjamin, ed. *Freud and the Twentieth Century*. New York: Meridian Books, Inc., 1957.

Nunberg, M. Herman & Federn, E., eds. *Minutes of the Vienna Psychoanalytic Society - Vols. 1 and 2*. Translated by M. Nunberg. New York: International Universities Press, 1962.

Ollman, Bertell. *Social and Sexual Revolution*. Boston: South End Press, 1979.

Peters, H.F. *My Sister, My Spouse*. New York: W.W. Norton & Co., Inc., 1962.

Puner, Helen Walker. *Freud - His Life and Mind*. New York: Charter Books, 1947.

Reich, Peter. *A Book of Dreams*. New York: Fawcett Publications, 1973.

Reich, Wilhelm. *The Function of the Orgasm*. New York: Pocket Books, 1973.

____. *The Mass Psychology of Facism*. Translated by Vincent R. Carfagno. New York: Farrar, Straus & Giroux, 1970.

____. *Sex-pol*. New York: Vintage Books, 1972.

____. *The Sexual Revolution*. Translated by Therese Pol. New York: Simon & Schuster, 1945.

Reiff, Philip. *Freud: The Mind of the Moralist*. Gardin City, NY: Doubleday & Co., Inc., 1961.

Rhode, Irma. *Viennese Cookbook*. New York: A. A. Wyne, Inc., 1951.

Rich, Alan. *The Simon & Schuster Listener's Guide to Opera*. New York: Simon & Schuster, 1980.

Roazen, Paul. *Brother Animal*. New York: Alfred A. Knopf, 1969.

____. *Freud and His Followers*. New York: New American Library, 1971.

Schorske, Carl. *Fin-de-Siecle Vienna*. New York: Alfred A. Knopf, 1980.

Schroeder, Joseph J., Jr. *Montgomery Ward & Co., 1894-95 Catalogue and Buyers Guide*. Northfield, IL: DBI Books, 1977.

Schur, Max , M.D. *Freud: Living and Dying*. New York: International Universities Press, 1972.

Sears, Roebuck & Co. *1909 Catalog*. New York: Ventura Books, Inc., 1979.

Stekel, Wilhelm. *Autobiography*. Edited by Emil A. Gutheil. New York: Liveright Pub. Co., 1950.

____. *The Interpretation of Dreams - New Developments and Techniques*. New York: Washington Square Press, 1967.

Stone, Irving. *The Passions of the Mind*. Garden City, NY: Doubleday & Co., Inc., 1971.

Stuhlmann, Gunther, ed. *The Diary of Anaïs Nin*. New York: Harcourt, Brace & World, Inc., 1966.

Sulloway, Frank J. *Freud, Biologist of the Mind*. New York: Basic Books, Inc., 1979.

Time-Life Books, eds. *This Fabulous Century, 1900 - 1910*. New York: Time-Life Books, 1969.

Virgil. *The Aeneid*. Baltimore, MD: Penguin Books, 1956.

Vollert, Jean. *Reluctant Feminists in German Social Democracy*.

Waissenberger, Robert. *Vienna 1890 - 1920*. New York: Tabard Press, 1984.

Waite, Arthur Edward. *The Book of Ceremonial Magic*. Secaucus, NJ: Citadel Press, 1973.

____. *The Holy Kabbalah*. Secaucus, NJ: University Books, Inc., 1975.

Walloman, Karl. *Family Encyclopedia*. Vienna, 1899.

Wittels, Fritz. *Biography of Sigmund Freud*. Leipzig: E. P. Tal Co., translated by Eden and Cedar Paul. London: George Allen & Unwin, 1924.

Wollheim, Richard. *Sigmund Freud*. New York: Viking Press, 1971.

Wortis, Joseph. *Fragments of an Analysis with Freud*. New York: Simon & Schuster, 1954.

Young-Bruehl, Elisabeth. *Anna Freud: A Biography.* New York:Summit Books, 1989.

*The Portable Jung.* Translated by R. F. C. Hull. Edited by Joseph Campbell. New York: Viking Press, 1971.

*The Complete Letters of Sigmund Freud to Wilhelm Fliess 1887-1904.* Translated and edited by Jeffrey Moussaieff Masson. Cambridge, MA: Belknap Press of Harvard University Press, 1985.